FALLING HARD

Eight Second Ride Book 1

I0520213

Sandy Sullivan

Erotic Romance

Secret Cravings Publishing
www.secretcravingspublishing.com

A Secret Cravings Publishing Book
Erotic Romance

Falling Hard
Copyright © 2015 Sandy Sullivan
Print ISBN: 978-1-63105-523-2

First E-book Publication: February 2015
First Print Publication: February 2015

Cover design by Dawné Dominique
Edited by Stephanie Balistreri
Proofread by Ariana Gaynor
All cover art and logo copyright © 2015 by Secret Cravings
Publishing

PUBLISHER
Secret Cravings Publishing
www.secretcravingspublishing.com

Dedication

This is dedicated to all the bull rider lovers out there.
We all like to watch the alpha males hang on for eight seconds.
I wanted to see what two of those would be like.
This is for all the people who love two hot guys together.

FALLING HARD
Eight Second Ride Book 1

Sandy Sullivan

Chapter One

"Now up, Levi Bond. Levi is an experienced rider on this bull. They've matched up before several times with Mr. Tough coming out on top every time. Levi needs this trip to be good to better his position for a run at the finals." The announcer's voice faded with the hush of the crowd.

A heavy coating of dust clung to everything. The crowd fell silent as the bull under him shifting nervously while he tried to get his bull rope just right before the gate opened for the eight seconds of craziness called bull riding. This ride meant everything. It could catapult him into the finals this year or leave him waiting in the wings.

He blew out a nervous breath.

The bull jumped. The spot man held onto his vest in case he needed to be pulled to safety.

Mr. Tough settled down although he continued to toss his head, banging his horns against the railing of the chute.

His spot man yelled the clock above his head had started, indicating he had thirty seconds to nod for them to open the chute. *Settle down, big boy.*

Sweat trickled down his back. His belly clenched. His heart raced. All of this for eight seconds on the back of a two-thousand pound animal who didn't want him there.

Levi twisted the rope around his hand, adjusted his position on the back of the bull and then nodded for them to open the gate.

Everything froze as the bull jumped straight up, twisting his body to the left, trying to dislodge the nuisance on his back. Levi adjusted as his left arm whipped back and forth, almost dislocating his shoulder in the process.

This was what he lived for, the adrenaline rush of bull riding.

Time stood still as the clock slowly ticked off the eight seconds he needed for this to be a qualifying ride.

The buzzer sounded.

He pulled the rope to release his hand and jump clear of the bull, who right now, wanted to gore him with his horns. His hand hung up in the rope.

The bull flung him to and fro like a ragdoll as the lights of the arena swirled around in his vision. His arm burned from being twisted. His stomach lurched with the pain of having his arm tangled in the rope. He felt his shoulder pop. *Shit.*

Finally, the bull fighter got his hand loose from the rope before he fell to the ground holding his useless arm.

When the bull had been corralled into the exit chute, the doctor rushed out. "Shoulder?"

"Yeah."

The doctor felt around the socket, pushing in a few spots. "Looks out of place. We'll pop it back in once we get you to the locker room. You really need to have surgery on this shoulder, Levi."

"I know. I can't yet though. Maybe in the off season."

The doctor grunted in response. Levi knew he wouldn't push the issue. Bull riders were a different breed. Tough as nails, bore more pain than the average person with grace and dignity, but were hard-headed and stubborn as a jackass. Levi grimaced at the pain shooting through his shoulder. Nothing new. Pain came with being a bull rider. "Thanks, Doc."

"No problem."

Climbing to his feet, he waved to the crowd to let them know he was okay and was meet with a resounding cheer. He glanced up at his score on the board before pumping his fist in the air. Ninety point seven five on his ride. That put him in first place for the weekend and gave him a good shot at going to the finals. Perfect.

With his right wrist held by his left hand, keeping the affected arm close to his body for support, he headed to the gate. Levi knew the drill. He'd dislocated this shoulder several times before, but he couldn't take the time off to get surgery on it. Taping it in place would have to do for now. The finals were coming up. He couldn't afford to be out the rest of the season. Luckily, he was done for the weekend here. The break coming up would be good enough to let his shoulder heal a little before the final push for finals in October. He needed to continue to ride well through the next several weeks to maintain his position to qualify.

As he came around the corner of the chutes to head to the locker room, he almost ran smack dab into fellow rider, Curt Walsh.

"You okay, Levi?"

"Yeah, popped my shoulder out again."

"Let Doc take care of you, and I'll see you later at the bar?"

"I'll be there. I'll need a few beers after this."

"Great ride, by the way."

"Thanks."

"I think you're gonna win this week."

"I hope so. I need all the points I can get to stay in the finals."

"Yeah, me too." Curt put his hand on Levi's shoulder. "See you in a little while."

Levi swallowed hard as shivers raced down his back. Curt was way out of his league even if he swung the same way Levi did and of that Levi didn't know. He'd seen Curt with a girl here and there, but he never seemed to hook up with one overnight or at least Levi had never seen one leave his room come morning. Hell, as far as he knew, Curt might be married although he didn't wear a wedding ring.

After he watched Curt walk back toward the chutes to catch the last few riders doing their thing, Levi followed Doc back toward the locker room. Ice and Ibuprofen would be on tap for tonight. Lots of it.

"Lie on the table, Levi, and we'll get this over with," Doc said, pointing to a gurney to his left, pushed up against the wall.

Levi stretched out on his back on the gurney as he blew out some slow, deep breaths to calm his heart. The thudding in his chest wasn't from the shoulder pain, it was from Curt. Damn, the man had it all. Tall, and built like a weightlifter with broad shoulders tapering to a trim waist, the man could make a girl or guy come in their pants with a simple look from those deep brown eyes. Dark hair hung in thick waves to his collar most of the time. Sleek hips gave away to long, firm legs encased in the standard Wranglers jeans finished off by worn cowboy boots. Curt could be the Marlboro Man if he wanted to. Stick a fork in Levi, he was done for.

The doc handed him four Ibuprofen, which he swallowed with a cup of water.

"Ready?"

"Yeah."

Doc Milburn took his hand and slowly pulled on his shoulder stretching the abused muscles until the shoulder popped back into place. *Easy peasy.*

"You know the drill, Levi. Wear the sling and get checked by your regular doctor soon. You shouldn't ride for a few weeks to give that shoulder time to rest."

"I know."

"But you won't listen to me even though I'm the doctor."

"I listen. I can't always follow your advice, Doc. You know how we are. You've been around the circuit long enough."

"I know all too well how bull riders are. That doesn't mean I don't tell you how to heal your body after you take falls that bust open your noggin, twist your arm until it breaks, or get stabbed by a bull's horns. I care about you guys." Levi sat up as Doc Milburn put the ice bag on his shoulder. "You should let me tape that."

"Okay."

Once the bag of ice was taped in place, Levi headed back out to see where he stood when everything was said and done. Only six riders needed to go after he hurt himself so they should be pretty much done for the night and he could relax a little. *Man, I need a beer.*

The closing ceremonies were about to get started when he got back to the rigging behind the chutes. The leader board flashed and he saw his time still held at number one for the weekend. He'd won! Thank God! He needed this win more than anything.

Curt walked up behind him, slapping him on his good shoulder. "You did well, man. First place for the weekend. Great win."

Levi exhaled sharply.

"Sorry. I didn't hurt you, did I?"

"No, I'm good." He wanted to turn around and press his mouth to Curt so bad, he could taste the man on his tongue. "Are you headed for the hotel?"

"Yeah, after we are done with meet and greets." The announcement was made on who took first place. "Your turn for glory, my man."

Levi nodded and hopped down so he could walk out in the arena to accept his belt buckle, along with the boots they got with every win from the boot maker. His check he would collect on the way out. The nice tidy sum this week would help with expenses. He needed it.

As they announced his name, he hopped up on the shark cage to wave his good hand at the crowd chanting and cheering his name. The sponsor held the belt buckle as they talked briefly about his injury and the win this week.

"How's your shoulder, Levi?"

"It'll be fine. I've dislocated it before."

"Are you going to be up for riding again in a couple of weeks? Your run for the finals hangs in the balance."

"I'll be ready. This won't hold me back."

"Well, good luck and we hope to see you in Vegas."

Levi took his buckle, held it high and pumped it into the air in celebration for his win before stepping down from the top of the shark tank and heading in the back to gather his stuff. He planned to put his gear in his room, take a quick shower, and hit the bar at the hotel where he knew the other riders would be. This was an every weekend occurrence for most of them. Those going home or heading to the next venue would drink their fill, sleep it off, and then hit the road the next morning.

Tonight he planned to celebrate with a lot of alcohol and maybe, just maybe, he might get lucky or numb himself to the point he didn't care anymore. Life was lonely for a cowboy on the circuit. Yeah, they could get women, more than their share most of the time, but that wasn't what drew him. He had a thing for cocks.

After he slipped the key into the lock of his room, he pushed open the door, dropped his gear on the floor, and then sat on the edge of the bed to pry off his boots. A heavy sigh escaped his lips as the boots slipped free. The small cloud of dirt that came with them would probably piss on the hotel staff who would have to vacuum, but oh well. He didn't have a choice. It came with riding bulls.

He slowly unwound the tape on his shoulder, releasing the bag of ice until it fell in a wet plop onto the bed next to his hip. He carefully rotated the shoulder, smiling when it didn't immediately pop back out. He'd be good to go after a shower.

His pants came next as he pushed them to the floor in a heap before removing his shirt in a slow, methodical movement so he wouldn't reinjure the ligaments barely holding the shoulder in place. Once he was buck-naked, he scratched a couple of places as he walked into the bathroom to turn on the shower. Hot water rushed from the nozzle the moment he turned on the spigot. As he stepped under the spray, he sighed, leaning back into the hot stream as he let it cascade over his head, washing away the sweat and grime of the day.

The heat felt heavenly, almost as good as sex. Okay, maybe not, but it did feel really good to have the water sluicing over his body as he stood there absorbing the heat from the shower. A couple of minutes later, he grabbed his shampoo and lathered his head before scratching his scalp to get all the dirt from it. He stepped back under the spray to rinse away the soap suds.

With a bar of soap in hand, he scrubbed his body to wash away all the grime from the arena in long slow strokes as he let his mind wander to Curt. He wanted the man, there was no doubt about that, but would he be able to have him. Oh well, Levi could always fantasize about him.

Letting the soap slick up his hand, Levi envisioned Curt on his knees in front of him in the shower. He fisted the other man's hair as Curt opened his mouth to take Levi's dick in a long, slow lick from balls to tip. He shuddered as shivers rolled down his back. Curt licked around the head, flicking his tongue relentlessly at the purple top. Levi moaned deep in his throat. His ass clenched wanting Curt to ream him hard, but first he needed this. The slow, aching sucking was driving him crazy.

With ball clenching precision, Curt pushed a finger into his ass as he licked and sucked the orbs of Levi's balls between his lips. Cum shot out the end of his dick without warning, coating his abdomen in stripes of white as he slumped against the cold tile of the shower, squeezing his eyes shut to try to calm his racing heart. His vision of Curt disappeared in a wisp of longing.

He exhaled on a rush, trying to bring his breathing back to normal before he soaped up again to rinse the cum from his abdomen. Getting himself off right now might keep him from jumping the man the next time he saw him, in a heated rush of need. Yeah, maybe not. He still wanted him with every fiber of his being.

When he finished cleaning himself up, Levi shut the water off, grabbed a towel from the rack hanging by the shower, and dried his skin.

A beer sounded really good at the moment, anything to numb the pain in his shoulder and the desire in his groin so he could sleep.

Fifteen minutes later found him strolling through the doors to the bar at the hotel. A sea of cowboy hats filled the area as he looked from one face to the other, trying to find someone he recognized. Several of the other bull riders leaned on the bar, sipping beers, so he headed in that direction.

The long mahogany sported a brass rail along the bottom, to rest your boots on as you sat at the bar. Rows of bottles graced the back bar with a huge mirror hanging there reflecting the hundreds of people talking and laughing. Everything from Jack Daniels to Wild Turkey could be had for a price. Levi wasn't in the mood for the hard stuff. A beer would do.

"Hey, Levi." A pretty blonde woman wrapped her arm around his waist and pulled him into a hug. "Busy tonight?"

"Uh, yeah."

"Oh, boo. I was hoping you would be available."

"Sorry, babe. With this shoulder, I'm out of commission for a couple of weeks."

"I bet your tongue still works, and I know mine does."

His dick didn't even twitch at the invitation on her lips or in her eyes. "Maybe some other time."

"Okay. Hey, if one of your friends might be interested, send them my way."

"Sure." *Buckle bunny to the core. Hopping from one bed to another depending on who is biting tonight.*

He walked up to the bar, signaling for a drink from the bartender.

"What would you like?"

"Bud, please."

"Sure. Bottle or draft?"

"Bottle is fine."

"Coming right up."

When the bartender brought back the bottle, Levi nodded in thanks, turned his back to the bar, and glanced around the room. A few of his fellow riders knew he was gay, but the majority of the fans and other riders on the circuit didn't know and he preferred it that way. His sexuality didn't have anything to do with the way he rode bulls. He would be judged though, he knew, and even a few of the riders would avoid him like the plague, so he kept quiet and did most of his playing at home in between stops on the circuit. It made for long spells of no sex, much to his dismay.

His gaze came to rest on the man sitting alone at a corner table. Curt. Damn, the man for being so gorgeous.

A woman approached and slid into the spot next to him. Curt drank his beer as the woman talked. She was very animated in her conversation, talking with her hands and laughing at whatever she was saying. Curt seemed disinterested, continuing to check out the huge television over the woman's shoulder to the left.

Levi could almost see the wheels turning in Curt's head to the tune of what might be going through his own should he be interested in women. *Yeah. Uh-huh. Nice. Score!* He tipped the bottle of beer to his lips, draining the last of the liquid from the brown glass before he signaled for the waitress to bring him another. The woman leaned in, burying her nose in Curt's neck. Curt smiled.

Maybe he did do women.

My loss.

Curt got a hand on the girl's shoulder and pushed her back with a frown.

Okay. Maybe not?

It looked as if Curt was reprimanding her. The woman frowned, got up and stomped away. Curt's gaze went back to the television. He knew the other man was a rabid sports fan so it didn't surprise him that Curt's attention was on the ESPN sports report.

Levi drank the rest of his beer before turning back to get another one from the bar. He wasn't sure he wanted to approach Curt tonight or not. After his fantasy in the shower, he might not be able to control himself around the guy. *Nah.* Tonight would be one of those nights he went to bed alone and woke up alone…again.

* * * *

Curt watched Levi from the corner of his eye as he tried to keep his focus on the sports program playing on the television. He wondered if his friend was in a lot of pain. He didn't appear to be, but he knew Levi well enough that, like any other rider, they hid their pain well. If Doc thought they were in too rough of a condition to ride, he made it well known they would be doing it against his advice.

He drained his beer and signaled for the waitress to bring him another. Tonight he wasn't in the mood for company of any sort. Thus, the reason he'd blown off the brunette who'd sat down with him. Not that she wasn't pretty or anything, but tonight he didn't feel up to entertaining.

His ride this weekend earned him a little cash. The big winner was Levi. He'd taken home the first prize for the week. *If I'm going to make finals, I need to get my shit together and ride.*

He hurt all over. His body telling him he needed a break. With only a few weeks left to qualify, he couldn't afford to stop. None of the riders could if they wanted to be in the finals. Vegas was coming up fast and furious.

Man, he wanted to go home for some rest. Texas called to him. The family place called to him. A break sounded wonderful and he knew his parents would like to see him. The finals screamed his name this year though. The ranch could wait. He had a good foreman and friend watching the place for him while he did his thing.

His heart felt heavy. Someday he wanted a partner, a spouse to run the place with him, but he knew that would be a long time coming. His preference in sexual partners made it difficult to settle down. He didn't want just one, he had a mind for two.

Curt didn't know Levi's sexual preferences, but he had an idea. They've never discussed it like so many men do on the circuit, but he'd also never seen Levi with a woman. Not that he couldn't be married or something and just didn't pickup buckle bunnies on a regular basis. Curt was almost sure Levi liked cock, funny thing was, so did he. He liked both actually. Pussy was nice on occasion too. There weren't too many women who got off seeing two guys together though. Any woman like that would be special, he knew. Oh well, he would know when the time was right if there was to be a woman in the mix. Right now, he wanted a nice tight asshole to plunder.

His gaze swung to Levi again as his friend leaned against the bar. Levi glanced his way and did the chin tip thing guys do as he raised his beer in salute. Curt waved him over. If nothing else, they could share a beer or two and go their separate ways at the end of the night, never knowing which way things might work should they actually discuss their sexual preferences in detail.

Levi pushed off the bar and sauntered toward him, his hips doing a slow shift as he walked. The man was built and ready for a ride if Curt knew anything at all. Tall at about six foot, broad in the shoulders and lean in the hips, he had the perfect body for a bull rider. His dark hair hung barely below his ears and his green eyes made Curt think of new sprouts. He wasn't sure what Levi's nationality was if anything other than white. His features didn't support any specific nationality like American Indian, African American or anything besides good old Caucasian.

Levi was good. He'd been on the circuit quite a few years, longer than Curt had been by just a few though. Curt joined the professional tour about five years past now and Levi had been one of the best even then. This year Levi had a chance at the world finals and so did Curt. They both were hoping for a string of good rides to keep them in the running for the title.

"What's up?" Levi ask, coming to a stop next to the table.

"Not much. You?"

"Nothing here either." Levi tipped his chin up. "Did you want me to join you?"

"Yeah. I figured you looked lonely over there all by yourself. I'm just sitting here chilling until my body unwinds from the adrenaline rush. Drinking a beer. Checking out the pickings in the bar. You know."

"Yep." Levi brought his beer to his lips, taking a couple of long swallows.

Curt swallowed hard as he watched the other man's Adams apple bob with each sip. His groin tightened uncomfortably behind the fly of his jeans. *Thank God, the table is hiding my hard-on.*

"You did awesome today on the back of that final bull. Great ride."

Levi set his beer on the table. "Thanks. You got a good score on yours too."

"Not good enough to beat you though."

Levi smiled, showing off a gorgeous grin. Curt had the insane urge to bite Levi's lower lip. The growl rumbling in his chest almost came out between his lips, but he managed to suppress it before he gave himself away. He wasn't sure he wanted to reveal his attraction to the other man, just yet.

He'd have to be careful. Gay action on the circuit could ruin a man's career if it ever got out. The other guys might be a bit weirded out if they found out one of their riding buddies was gay or bi-sexual as in his case.

"Are you going home between weekends?" Levi asked, sipping his beer again.

"No. You?"

"After this weekend coming up, yeah. Home isn't too far away from where we'll be."

"Where are you from?"

"Oklahoma. You?"

"Texas. Amarillo."

"Well hell. I'm from a little town north of Oklahoma City. Near Stillwater called Mystique."

"We are practically neighbors."

"Yep." Curt brought the beer bottle to his lips for a long drink before sitting it back down on the table top. "Do you have a place there?"

"Yeah. Some land I run horses on, breed cattle, and hope to raise some bucking bulls soon."

"You raise horses, but you ride bulls?"

Levi grinned as he swirled the dregs of his beer around in the bottom of the bottle. "Sure do. I love horses. I do have a couple of bulls too, but I don't do much with them except practice rides."

"Hell, I thought every bull rider wanted to raise bucking bulls."

"Do you?"

"Nope. I would like to raise beef cattle someday when I retire from bull riding."

"Do you have a place to call home?"

"Not really. I have a small place on my parent's property when I'm there. Being on the road so much, there isn't much reason to have a place."

"My parents have a place near mine. I grew up in the same neighborhood I have my ranch on now. I bought my place from an old family friend when they decided to retire from ranching, travel the country in their motorhome, you know."

"What's it like?"

"Five hundred acres of prime grazing land. Nice little three bedroom ranch house with a porch goin' all the way around. A big red barn in the distance."

The faraway look in Levi's eyes told Curt he loved his place almost as much as bull riding, which would be a tremendous amount because Levi loved bull riding. "Sounds like a great place."

"It is. I'd show you a picture, but I don't have anything on me. My phone is charging in my room."

"Too bad. I would love to have seen it."

"Maybe at our next stop I can show you some of the shots I have. It's a great place."

"That would be great, Levi."

Levi signaled the waitress over and ordered two more beers. "So. Anyone catch your attention tonight?"

"Not really."

"I saw the chick comin' onto you pretty strong a little bit ago."

"Yeah, not my type."

"What is your type?"

Chapter Two

Curt drank the last of his beer before shoving the bottle into the middle of the table. "Oh, I don't know. I like a lot of different types. I'm not sure I have just one."

"Come on. What do you prefer then? Blondes, brunette, red-head? Tall, short, skinny, curvy?"

"I like them all."

"Hmm."

The waitress arrived with their beers, Levi paid for this round. He would get the next one. "How about you? You got a preference?"

Levi's gaze shifted around before coming back to Curt as he leaned in and rested his elbows on the table. "I can't say that I do."

"See. You're in the same boat I am."

"Yeah, I guess so."

"I'm just not in the mood for pussy tonight."

Levi's eyebrow shot up over his left eye. "Oh?"

"Nope."

"I couldn't anyway with this bum shoulder. It makes it really hard to get horny when you're hurting."

The furrowing of Levi's eyebrows told him he was in more pain than he was willing to admit probably. "Are you in a lot of pain?"

"Not so much now, but if I tried getting laid tonight, I'd probably be doubled over in the corner." Levi leaned back in his chair, lifting it so he balanced only on the back legs. "Why aren't you in the mood tonight?"

"Just not, I guess." Shrugging, he glanced at the television, noting the scores he watched regularly. His gaze rested back on Levi a minute later. They were dancing around each other, sparring so to speak, neither of them willing to admit they wanted more than pussy tonight. Oh well, he'd survive. He didn't want to pressure his friend into something he didn't want or couldn't do. It wasn't right. If they were meant to have sex, they would— eventually.

The bar seemed to be getting louder as people continued filing in. It was Saturday night, after all. The crowd didn't surprise him a bit. Lights blinked in a strange pattern on the various beer signs hanging in different area of the bar. The group of bull riders hung out in several groups, many looking to hook up with a buckle bunny to warm their beds for the night. The long mahogany bar was the spot where most of them hung out in rows and rows of Wranglers lined up in a fine display of cowboy ass. There were cowboy hats galore in the place, everything from Stetson to straw graced the heads of most of the men and even some of the women. You could tell the wannabes from the real riders by the dirt clinging to their boots.

He took a swallow of his beer, glancing across the table at Levi while he wondered what made the man tick. He'd known Levi for several years, but he didn't *know* him the way he wanted to. The inkling of which way Levi swung was a rumor going around the riders, but no one knew for sure. Levi kept that part of his life to himself.

"What?" Levi asked.

"I'm just trying to figure you out."

Levi shrugged as he took another swig from the beer in his hand. "Nothing much to know. I'm a bull rider. We have hard heads, a stubborn streak a mile wide, we love hard when we fall, and we don't like being told no."

Curt chuckled at Levi's description. It fit the two of them to a T. "Are you going to rest that shoulder?"

"Can't. I have to keep my points up to qualify for the world finals. You know that."

"I know. I thought I'd ask, is all."

"I appreciate it."

"You need surgery."

"Yeah, eventually. I'll just have Doc tape it up good before the next several rides. Finals aren't too far away and then I can have surgery when we are finished riding."

"Where are you standing right now?" Curt asked, even though he knew exactly where Levi sat in the standings. He'd been keeping a close eye on his friend for several weeks.

"Thirty-five so I'm in as long as I hold my points. You?"

"Thirty-six. I need some good rides in the next three weeks to get in."

"Vegas is a fun town. Lots to do."

"Definitely."

Levi peeled the label off his bottle slowly, concentrating on making sure it didn't rip. Music thumped from the speakers, almost giving Curt a headache along with his blue balls. His body was beginning to feel every jerk the bull made, and the hard landing he'd taken tonight, right into the dirt. Ibuprofen would be on the menu before he hit the sack.

"So, you ever been in love?" Levi asked, his gaze intent on Curt's.

"Nope. You?"

"Nope."

Two ladies wandered over to their table. "Mind if we join you, gentlemen?"

Levi looked at him. He shrugged, indicating he didn't care one way or another. *This might make for interesting conversation later.* "Please, sit down."

"My name is Marie and this is Sondra." The blonde indicated herself before pointing to her friend.

They were like night and day, one being light haired and the other being dark haired. He didn't care. He wasn't picky when it came to a woman.

"Nice to meet you, ladies." Levi tipped his hat. "Would you like a drink?"

"That would be great," Sondra answered as Levi signaled for the waitress.

Once their order had been taken, the women started asking questions about both of them. "Are you two some of the bull riders in town for the rodeo this weekend?"

"Yes, ma'am, but it's not a rodeo, it's the bull riders association event."

Maria's eyebrows furrowed. "What's the difference?"

"Our event is only bull riding. Rodeos have all different events like calf roping, steer wrestling, barrel racing, and bronc riding."

"I still don't get it." Sondra frowned before taking a drink of her beer.

"We get on bulls, ride for eight seconds, and then get off. The other events don't happen at a bull riding association events," Curt answered.

"Were you ladies at the event tonight?"

"No," Maria replied. "We heard about it, but we both had to work late so we couldn't go. We wanted to though, you know, to meet the riders and stuff."

"Where do you ladies work?" he asked, trying to keep the conversation going even though Levi didn't seem the least bit interested in the two women.

"At the hospital. We are both nurses on the cardiac floor."

"Most of the riders are here at the bar. You could meet almost everyone if you went around the room." Levi took a drink of his beer, draining the bottle in a couple of gulps.

"Really?"

"Yeah. I'm Levi Bond." He pointed to Curt. "This is Curt Walsh."

"It's nice to meet you both." Sondra looked Levi straight in the face. "Are you two up for a little rodeo action tonight?"

"No thanks," Levi was quick to answer. "I hurt my shoulder tonight. I'm out for the count for a couple of weeks."

The two women looked shocked before they turned their attention to him. "What about you, handsome? A little ménage action maybe?"

"Maybe."

Levi's right eyebrow shot up over his eye as he gave Curt a questioning look.

What the hell? I might as well get something tonight since it doesn't appear I'll be going backdoor with him. Curt drained his beer. "Let me pay my tab and we'll head on upstairs."

Both women grinned as he got to his feet, revealing the hard-on behind his fly. They didn't have to know it wasn't for them. He ambled over to the bar, paid his tab and then walked back to the table. "Shall we?"

The women drained their drinks in two quick gulps, before they stood. Both wobbled a little as they swayed toward him. *Great. They're both a little drunk on top of everything. Oh well, I'll get laid and we'll worry about the rest later.* "Follow me, ladies." He tipped his hat to Levi. "Catch you later."

"Have fun."

He weaved his way through the throng of people with a girl on each arm. Two pussies didn't equal Levi's cock, but he would make do, he figured.

The girls giggled when he led them toward the elevator. Sondra pushed the button as he glanced at each one in turn. Sondra had a bigger chest than Marie, but Marie was taller. He wouldn't mind being sandwiched between the two or watching a little girl on girl action. The suggestion had merit as far as he was concerned.

The doors opened revealing several of the other bull riders coming down to the bar. He got several grins and good luck wishes from them as they kept going.

Once they reached the floor where his room was, he slipped the card into the door, watching as the light turned green.

He ushered the girls inside the room. The whole place went dark when the door clicked shut behind them, except for a small sliver of light revealed by the slightly parted curtains. "Hang on. Let me get the lamp." As the light illuminated the room, he cringed. He had stuff lying everywhere from his dirty jeans to his chaps across the chair. "Let me just straighten this up a little."

When he glanced back to where the women had been standing, he was intrigued to see them lying across the bed, touching each other. His night just got a whole lot better.

* * * *

Levi rolled out of bed the next morning with a whole lot of stuff on his mind. He hadn't slept well because of his shoulder pain and the ache in his balls from hanging with Curt the night before. His head didn't feel a whole lot better either after downing several shots of whiskey to try to dull the ache in his dick. Horny wasn't an effective way of putting it. His cock burned from the raging hard-on he'd had since Curt walked away with the two women. Normally, he couldn't get excited around women, but the thought of Curt banging those two and then reaming him? Holy shit!

Hmm. That's a thought to be thinking this morning.

Once he got to his feet, he raked his fingers through his hair realizing he needed a shower. The stench of beer and whiskey on his skin almost made him gag. He hadn't even taken off his pants last night before he passed out in the bed, just unbuttoned them, letting the denim hang open at the waist, and the legs drag on the floor.

A rap of knuckles on the door startled him. Who would be knocking on his door this morning? All of the riders would be pulling out, headed for next weekend's venue.

"Yeah?"

"It's me, Curt."

"Just a second." Figuring to hell with his attire, he pulled open the door to find the sexy dark-haired bull rider leaning on his forearm with his head bent. Levi couldn't see Curt's face from where he stood, but the broad shoulders encased in the worn western style shirt, jeans, and boots personified cowboy. "What's up?"

Curt lifted his head and Levi could see the shit eating grin on the other man's face when he tilted his head to the side, giving Levi a slow, perusal from the top of his head to the bare feet on the floor. "Am I bugging you?"

"No. I was getting in the shower."

One eyebrow rose as the grin turned into a sexy twist of his lips. Levi wanted to yank him by the shirtfront into the room with him, shuck his clothes then drag his naked ass into the shower and fuck him like tomorrow didn't matter.

"Uh, did you need something?"

"I thought you might want to get some breakfast before we head out? I figured we could convoy to the next stop. Maybe share a room at the next hotel. These bills are killing me." He leaned in to look past Levi toward the inside of the room. "Don't you usually share with someone?"

He didn't want to tell Curt he didn't like sharing a room with anyone in case he found someone he wanted to hook up with for the night. The fact of his sexual preferences didn't need to get around the circuit. He wanted to keep it on the down low if at all possible. "No. I snore like a freight train so most guys don't want to room with me."

"I don't mind. I have earplugs. One of my other roomies I used to share with snored like that."

"Well, I'm not sure that is a good idea?"

"Why the hell not?"

Levi couldn't think of a good excuse so he just shrugged. "Let me get a quick shower and I'll meet you downstairs for breakfast. We can figure it out when we get to the next stop."

"Sounds good."

"Did you get rid of the girls early or late last night?"

"I'll tell you all about it at breakfast."

"Sounds good. I'll be down in about fifteen."

"Okay. Do you want coffee?"

He rotated his shoulder, groaning softly when the muscles burned with the movement. "Yeah, and lots of it. My shoulder burned most of the night. I didn't get a lot of sleep."

"I'll get them to bring a pot to the table." Curt stepped back. "See you in a few."

"Sure."

Levi shut the door, turning so his back was to the cool exterior and sighed. The last thing he needed this morning was Curt. Well, that wasn't exactly true. He needed the other man more than his next breath, but what he didn't need was to have to stare across the table at him wishing he could climb under the table to suck him off while people milled around them. He just didn't have the willpower where Curt was concerned, to tell the man no under any circumstances. Should he asked for sex, Levi would be there in a heartbeat.

After a second or two, he pushed off the doorframe and headed for the bathroom. A cold shower might do him good right now. The small shower wouldn't have worked very well for great shower sex anyway, but man, he could wish, hope, and dream, couldn't he?

About twenty minutes later, he found himself standing in the hotel lobby. The café was to his right. He could see Curt sitting near the window nursing a cup of coffee, another steaming cup sitting in front of the empty seat across from him. Levi willed his soft cock to behave around the other man and walked toward the seating area. Curt turned his dark eyed gaze on him and smiled. Levi almost tripped over his own feet. If he didn't know better, he could almost believe Curt was attracted to him. *Nah. Can't be. Curt likes women, right?* He did take two back to his room last night and presumably had sex with them, right?

"There you are." He did the chin tip thing indicating Levi should sit in the chair across from him. "I didn't know how you took your coffee, so there is cream and sugar up there near the salt."

"Thanks."

"Sure. No problem."

When Levi had finished doctoring his coffee, he stirred the now light brown liquid, the spoon clinking against the side of the cup. He didn't glance up as he fought to control his thoughts from revealing themselves in his gaze when he finally faced the tempting man across from him.

"Didn't sleep well, eh?"

Levi sighed as he lifted his gaze. *Damn, the man is hot.* "No, not really. Shoulder bugged me most of the night. It's kind of stiff this morning." *That's not the only thing stiff.* He discreetly adjusted his cock in his jeans. Even the smell of the guy drove him crazy.

A little smile lifted the corners of Curt's mouth.

Curt had to know what he was doing to him, didn't he?

"Well, the girls left early this morning. I guess it was more like the middle of the night but it was a great night."

Levi really didn't want to hear about Curt sleeping with women when he wanted the man for himself, but it was what it was. Conversations like this always happened around the circuit. Levi learned to live with it from early on. "Oh?"

"Yeah, I didn't realize it, but the girls were bi. They were having a lot of fun getting it on together. I watched."

"You didn't participate?"

"A little, but it was better watching them." Curt leaned in. "I jacked off while they were all over each other on the bed."

He could feel a frown pulling down the corners of his mouth. He wasn't sure how fun that would have been.

"What?"

"I guess if that's what gets you off, then so be it."

Curt made a little snorting noise, but let the conversation drop. "Are you going to be ready for the next round with that shoulder?"

"I'm going to have them ice it down real good before we ride and try to keep it tucked into my body. It's the best I can do until we reach the end of season break in a couple of weeks and I can have it looked at."

"How the hell are you going to ride in the finals with it like that?"

"Very carefully."

"You're an idiot."

He lifted his coffee to his lips to take a sip of the hot liquid. "I'm riding in the finals. I need to do well this year. I can't be out because of a stupid injury."

Curt's fingers played with the handle on his cup. "That's your riding hand, isn't it?"

"Yeah, so? I can switch if I need to and ride left handed."

The other man's eyebrows dipped down between his eyes as a frown settled on his face. "What's got you so determined to ride until the end? You should be taking care of that shoulder so you don't ruin your career all together."

"I have my place to take care of me for the rest of my days, but this is a chance to win the world championship. I can't let that go. It's been a goal of mine since I started this ride."

"I understand that, Levi, really I do. I know what it's like to have that goal, but your health has to come first if you plan to continue after this year."

Levi let his good shoulder lift and fall in a shrug. "Maybe I don't."

"You're going to retire after finals?"

"I don't know. I might if I go out on top."

"Wow."

"How long do you plan to ride, Curt?" he asked, wondering what the man's plans were for the rest of his life. *Why should I care? It's not like we are best friends or anything else.* He did care though for some weird reason. Curt had been more of a friend than anyone else on the circuit in recent months. Levi had always kept to himself a bit, not wanting the other guys to get wind of his sexual preferences or make them uncomfortable thinking he had the hots for them when he didn't. Most of the guys, he wasn't attracted to. Curt? Yeah, he would do him in a New York minute.

"Until I can't anymore, I guess. Bull riding is my life."

"Mine too."

Silence fell between them as Levi wondered what the next few weeks would bring. His shoulder he could live with, but the attraction to the man across from him would drive him nuts in the long run, especially if he didn't get some relief soon.

"So how do you want to do this?"

"Do what?"

"I thought we could caravan to the next venue, maybe share a room? I really need to cut back on expenses since I didn't place this week."

Levi debated on how this would work out. Living in the same room with a man he was hot for would be torture. Unfortunately, yeah, he could use the break in expenses too. "Sounds fine to me."

"Great! We can have breakfast before we get on the road. The next stop is a couple days drive from here unless we drive straight through. Of course, that just means spending a couple of days there before the round begins. We do have some promotional stuff to do for the circuit, I believe, signings and appearances."

"I know. I wish they would have scheduled these a little closer to together, but after the next round I can go home for a couple days since this one is in Oklahoma."

"California to Oklahoma is about twenty-five hours straight through."

"I'm thinking we should take our time."

"Sounds good to me." The waitress came by to take their order for breakfast. "Uh, two eggs, over medium, bacon, hash browns and toast, please."

"Same for me," Levi said as he folded the menu and handed it back to her. When she walked away, he took up the conversation again. "Are you sure you want to room with me?"

A twinkle appeared in Curtis gaze. "Sure. Why wouldn't I?"

"Well, as I mentioned, I snore pretty badly."

"I can handle it."

Without any other excuse to use, Levi fell silent as he contemplated how hard this would be. Sleeping, showering, and hanging out with Curt every day from now until at least the end of the next venue?

"I was thinking we could make this a permanent arrangement."

"Permanent as in how?"

"At least until the end of the season. I mentioned these expenses are killing me and I'm sure they are you too. Although, you won this weekend, so you should be sitting pretty for now."

"Yeah, but with my ranch, a lot of the money I earn has to go to making sure my animals are fed, the mortgage is paid, and my hands receive their salaries."

"I bet it's an expensive endeavor."

"Sometimes, but it's totally worth it in the long run. I love having my own ranch. I hope to have some prime bucking bulls in a couple of years too."

"You're going to become a contractor when you retire?"

"Yeah, that's the plan even though I still have cattle to sell at market, horses I'm raising and training for bronc riding. I'm also training cutting horses."

"Wow. You've got it all going on there. Anyone special you are sharing it with?"

"Nope. I'm not married or with anyone at the moment."

Curt tipped his head to the side and nodded. "It's hard when we are gone so much."

"Yeah. I don't know how the wives do it with the guys gone so much. Traveling over two hundred days out of the year sucks."

"It would almost be better to bring your spouse or significant other along."

"What about when they have kids or a place to maintain? That doesn't work too well either."

"True."

Their breakfast arrived minutes later and while Levi ate, he contemplated what Curt had said. Someday he wanted someone to share his place with, someone to wake up to every morning, to drink coffee with, to share the good times and bad, but he wasn't sure it would ever happen. It wasn't everyday one took another man as a spouse. The town of Mystique, Oklahoma didn't seem to accommodating when it came to alternate lifestyles.

Levi discreetly watched Curt as he ate his food. His fingers were long with blunt cut fingernails. The bronze skin tone told Levi he either spent a lot of time in the sun or had some other heritage than just Caucasian, maybe Indian from some past relative. His had the high cheekbones, but he wasn't lanky. Levi sighed. He knew he was attracted to Curt from the moment they met a few years ago. Keeping that attraction to himself was difficult and getting harder every day, especially when Curt insisted they now room together.

"Do you have a lot to pack?" Curt asked, taking the last bite of his eggs before pushing his plate away.

"No. Just my gear bag and the few pairs of clothes I brought. Two bags at most. I can be ready in about five minutes."

"Good. We should probably hit the road soon if we want to take our time getting there."

"Yeah." Levi finished his breakfast with a last swipe of the fork across the plate to pick up the remaining hash browns.

The waitress brought their tab. Levi grabbed it to pay for both their meals. It was the least he could do since he won the night before. "I got it."

"I'll get mine, Levi."

"I said, I got it. I won. I can pay for breakfast. You can get tomorrow."

"Fine." Curt stood, finishing his coffee in one tip of the cup to his lips. "I'll meet you down here in fifteen minutes so we can get moving."

"Sounds good." Levi watched Curt's ass as he walked away, thinking all the while how he wanted to plunder that puckered little hole so bad, his balls ached. *Get over it. He's not into guys, he's into women.*

Jefferson Thompson stopped at the table before Levi could get up to leave. "Hey, Bond. What's between you and Curt? You two look awfully chummy lately. You banging him or something?"

Chapter Three

"Fuck you, Jefferson. What I do is my own business and no, I'm not banging him." Levi stood to his full height of six two, towering over the shorter man. "What business is it of yours? Besides, he had two women in his room last night, so yeah, who was banging who? I didn't see you taking two women back to your room."

Jefferson paled. "I…uh."

"Yeah, that's what I thought." Levi grabbed the check and headed to the cashier's station to the left. He just wanted to pay the bill and get the hell out of there. He hated Jefferson Thompson with a passion, but to have the man question his sexual preference hit a little too close to home. He'd have to be more careful. *Having breakfast with someone doesn't mean a damned thing anyway. Lots of the guys travel together and room together to save on costs.*

Levi didn't want things to get out into the circuit. If they did, it would make things difficult for him, he figured. You didn't hear about bull riders being gay, not on this circuit anyway.

After he paid his check, he headed for the elevator to grab his gear. He didn't carry much with him when he traveled. A few changes of clothes, his bull rope, rosin, private items like shampoo, conditioner, soap, laundry detergent, and other personal care items made up the main staples of his stuff.

He got off the elevator on his floor, walked to his room, slid the key card into the lock, and pushed open the door. The room was a typical motel room. Nothing much to write home about with the white bedspread, brown carpet, and it's equally ugly curtains on the window. Someday, he would be able to afford a suite, he hoped.

The door banged shut behind him as he moved to grab his dirty socks from the floor so he could stuff them into his duffle. His riding supplies were already in his gear bag. He checked the room one last time for anything he missed, opened the door and ran smack into Cyrus Cochran. "Hey, Cyrus."

"What's up, Levi?"

Levi shrugged as he set his bag on the floor to check the door. "Not much. Getting ready to roll out to Oklahoma for the next stop."

"Yeah, me too." He glanced over Levi's frame. "You riding with someone?"

"Curt and I are convoying. If you want to tag along, you can, I suppose. We are taking our time though. Stopping at a hotel tonight."

"Nah, that's okay. I have family to stay with in Phoenix. Good luck on the next round. You did well this weekend."

"Thanks. I just hope my shoulder holds up."

"That's right. You dislocated it, didn't you?"

"Yep. It's sore, but it's okay."

"Your riding hand right?"

Levi nodded. "It'll be okay though. I'm babying it right now so it'll be okay for this weekend."

"Aren't you close to qualifying for finals?"

He nodded again. "I need to win this weekend to qualify. With the last run coming up in a month, I need all the points I can get."

Cyrus tipped his hat. "Well, good luck to you. I'll see you in Oklahoma."

"Thanks."

Cyrus went on down the hall, the clank of his boots muffled by the carpet on the floor. Levi picked up his bag before he headed for the elevator to meet Curt in the lobby. They needed to get moving. It was almost ten already and with a twenty-five plus hour drive in front of them, they had to put some miles on the tires before nightfall. They could drive late if they wanted to, but Levi needed to rest his shoulder more than not. Driving might aggravate it a bit.

When the elevator doors opened, he spotted Curt lounging next to a large white pillar, his bags at his feet. "You ready?"

"Yeah, let's roll."

"Do you have a GPS so we know where we are going?"

"Yep. I've already got the information written down so I just need to plug it in when I get to my truck and we'll be all set."

"Great."

The two of them walked down the long hall toward the parking garage of the hotel. Levi had a large dually pickup he loved.

"I have a small ford ranger truck. Green. I'll meet you out by the curb. I'm up on the second level," Curt said as they parted ways at the doors.

"I'm driving a black dually. You'll hear me coming from a mile away. It's a diesel."

Curt laughed. The deep, rich baritone of his laughter caught Levi by surprise. The sound traveled straight to his dick, getting a huge rise out of the offending member that had a mind of its own where Curt was concerned. Luckily, Curt had already walked away and didn't see the hard-on Levi now sported. *Damn thing.*

Levi found his truck a minute later, tossed his bags in behind the seat, and then climbed in behind the wheel. The truck started with a low growl. Man, he loved that sound. He programmed the address for the venue into his GPS, and waited for it to finish computing before he backed out of the parking spot.

He pulled out of the garage just as Curt pulled in behind him at the gate releasing them from their concrete prison for vehicles.

It took a couple of minutes for them to get onto the highway headed out of town. Once underway, he popped in his iPod, got the music started, and settled in for the long ride.

* * * *

Curt watched the back of Levi's truck in the distance as they drove on through the day. The truck was just like its owner, big, built, and bad or at least he wanted to think so. Levi was an enigma to him at the moment. He wasn't sure which was the guy swung, but he had a feeling it was with others of his own sex. Good. Curt wanted to find out just how hard the guy swung. Now his own preferences ran both ways, but he really liked plundering a man's asshole and Levi was the one he wanted to ream. "Maybe tonight, my friend. Maybe tonight." He definitely had ulterior motives for asking Levi to share a room with him. It would be easier to seduce the man if they were together nonstop, he figured. His cock swelled behind the fly of his jeans as he adjusted himself to relieve some of the pressure.

Thoughts of Levi going down on him had him hard in seconds. Levi had a sweet mouth just made to fuck. As soon as he double-checked on the other man's preferences, all bets were off. They'd be fucking like bunnies before finals, he hoped.

Levi was six-foot-two of pure muscle as were most bull riders. His green eyes reminded Curt of grass swaying in the summer sun. Blond hair framed his face, but he kept the locks short in the back. He usually wore a straw cowboy hat when he rode although he switched out for a helmet here lately after one of their fellow riders was almost killed riding without a helmet. Curt was glad he'd switched.

His friend was on fire with his rides lately. Last weekend he'd went dead on, riding all of his bulls with precision and grace. Every bull rider on the circuit probably wished they could ride the way Levi rode. He definitely earned his check.

They were both riding for the finals in October. They only had a few more events to make sure their points were enough to get them in. Levi was on the edge. Him? He still had to win an event or at least come in a good second to get close. It wasn't the end of the world if he didn't make it, but he had a feeling for Levi, it might be.

Curt frowned when he thought about Levi retiring. The man was good, damn good. If he retired after this year, they would be losing one of the best riders on the circuit, but Curt would also be losing someone he'd learned a lot from, grown to admire, and one of the kindest guys he knew. Levi would do anything to help if someone was down. He'd been known to give other guys money, if they were going to have to sleep in their vehicle, so they could get a hotel room or buy someone a meal if they were sitting one out because they couldn't afford it that week.

The blinker on Levi's truck came on as they neared an exit. His friend probably needed to take a leak or something. Curt followed him off the exit to the truck stop a block away. Levi pulled up to the gas pump to fill up as Curt pulled in behind him. He might as well get gas too. Levi's truck would take a lot more fuel than his to get to Oklahoma.

"I need to get something to eat soon. Do you want to eat here or find somewhere else to sit down up the road? There is a restaurant here that doesn't look too bad we could try," Levi said from the rear of his truck as the tank filled.

"Sure. We've been on the road for several hours. I could use a stretch. I'm sure you need the break too with that shoulder."

Levi slowly rotated his shoulder as he held onto the top of his bicep with his good hand. "Yeah. It hasn't been bad, but the constant sitting is getting rough on the ass. Even though I have good seats, things still tend to fall asleep after a while."

Curt grinned. He would love to massage the feeling back into Levi's ass, preferably as he fucked him hard from behind. "I know what you mean. My little truck is great on gas mileage, but hard on the ass."

The gas pump clicked off on Levi's truck. Curt's had already finished filling. "How about we eat here."

"Sure."

They both found a parking spot not far from each other. As he walked out to meet Levi, he wondered what the coming night would bring. He knew they were going to stop somewhere halfway for the night before driving the other twelve plus hours on into Oklahoma. Did Levi sleep in the buff? What would it be like to shower with him? They could soap each other up real well, making their bodies all slick to the touch. He would love to run his hands over Levi's cock and balls, his touch working the other man into a frenzy of need.

Curt cleared his throat. No use getting ahead of things just yet.

Once inside, the waitress showed them to a booth where they slid in and got comfortable. He checked out the menu before deciding on a bacon cheeseburger and fries. "What are you having?"

"Hot roast beef sandwich, I think. You?"

"My old standby, bacon cheeseburger. I love those things."

Levi folded the menu and set it to his right. "You don't have to worry about cholesterol, so yeah, go for it."

"Why do you say that?"

"Because I'm about five years older than you are, and I have a family history of heart disease. I really need to watch what I eat before my arteries get so clogged, I croak out in the back of the chutes somewhere from a heart attack."

"Oh please. You are in great shape. I bet you work out daily."

The waitress came by, took their drink order and said she would return in a moment to get their food order.

Levi shrugged his good shoulder, giving Curt the impression he was still hurting quite a bit as he babied the bad one. "I try to, but there isn't always a gym available in these hotels. Do you work out?"

"Yeah, some. I'm not into heavy training since I do a lot of that on the bulls, but I try to keep up with weights so my arms stay strong."

"I need to do more shoulders and arms. I can't though now, until after I have this one looked at to see if there is anything they can do for it."

"You've probably stretched or torn some ligaments in there."

"Probably."

The waitress dropped off their drinks before taking their food order. "Anything else I can get you guys for now?"

"I think we are all set for now."

"All right. I'll be back when the food is ready. It shouldn't take long. It's not terribly busy yet."

"Great. Thanks."

She gave him a little shy smile as he smiled back. She was kind of cute with blonde bouncy curls, pretty blue eyes, pink lips meant for kissing, and tits that would stop traffic. He glanced across the table at Levi as the other man ignored the waitresses flirting. Yep, if he pegged him right, Levi was a full blown, flying under the radar, gay man. "So, what kinds of things do you like to do on your time off?"

"What time off? If I'm not riding, I'm training to ride, working my ranch, or training to ride some more. It's a never ending thing. I have some bulls on my ranch I use to train with as well as a barrel to work. I never have time off."

"True. I can see your point." He leaned in, resting his elbows on the table. "What do you like to do for fun?"

"Play pool, read, ride horses on the property, go camping. You know, things like that."

"Guy things."

"Yeah, I guess you could call them guy things."

"Hmm. Just curious."

"What kind of stuff do you do in your free time?"

"Same things mostly. I tinker around in my garage. I have an old '65 Mustang I'm fixing up."

Levi whistled in appreciation. "I love Mustangs."

"Me too." He tapped his fingers together. "I ride my motorcycle when I have time and the weather is nice."

"Didn't you say you lived on your parents place?"

"Yeah. I have a small house on their property where I live. It used to be the foreman's place, but he got married a few years ago and moved in town with his wife. He still works the home place, but he doesn't live on it anymore."

"Interesting arrangement."

"Yeah, it works. I get a place to crash and be near the folks so it works for me."

"Are you close to your parents?"

"Yeah, pretty close."

The waitress brought their food. Levi's roast beef looked really good for it coming from a greasy truck stop diner. He glanced down at his bacon cheeseburger as his mouth began to water. Everything looked very tasty and he hoped it tasted as good as it looked.

With some ketchup and mayo on the bun, he pushed the top bun down to squish it together so he could get his mouth around it, before lifting it to his mouth to take a healthy bite. He groaned as the burger, cheese, and mixings hit his taste buds. "This is really good," he said around the food in his mouth. "How's yours?"

Curt watched as Levi slid the tinges of his forks between his lips. He couldn't remember when he'd seen something so sexy. He couldn't wait to get those lips wrapped around his cock.

"You okay?" Levi asked, taking a sip of his Coke.

Curt cleared his throat. "Yeah. I'm fine. Why?"

"You were staring."

Levi took another bite of his food before licking the fork clean. Curt almost groaned in response to the sexy sight. "Sorry. I was thinking."

"Anything specific you were thinking about?"

Yeah, you sucking my cock. "Not really. Just mentally getting ready for this weekend, I guess. I need to place well, otherwise, I'll be out of the finals."

"You did pretty good last weekend in the points run."

"I gained some leverage against some of the runners, yes, but I need to do better."

"Me too. I'm hanging on by a thread."

"With only a few weeks left in the running, I need every point I can get. If I draw some rank bulls, keep my ass on them, and get some great rides, I can qualify."

Levi pushed his now empty plate away before drinking the last of his Coke. Curt really hoped they could make some headway into the bedroom tonight, but he wasn't sure. Levi didn't seem all that interested in him. He would really have to find out before he made any kind of move on his friend, otherwise he could ruin a really good friendship. This one seemed to be working out rather nice, but if Levi wasn't gay, any move on his part could really blow up in his face.

The waitress stopped at their table. "Can I get you boys anything else?"

"The bill would be great."

She pulled the paper from her pocket and slid it to the center. Curt grabbed it before Levi could do anything with it. "My turn. You got breakfast."

"All right."

"How much further are we going to drive tonight?"

"I'm thinking another four or five hours ought to do it. That'll put us about half way there and we can drive in the rest of the way tomorrow."

Curt nodded. "Sounds good to me."

Curt paid their bill and shortly afterward they were back on the road with him following Levi's truck down the interstate.

The slow uphill climb outside of Flagstaff, Arizona signaled their stop for the night. They'd agreed it was about halfway and a good place to end their trek for the day. Curt groaned as they pulled off the freeway. He wasn't sure where Levi planned to stay, but right now he wanted to get out of his truck, stretch his legs, and get the feeling back in his ass.

They pulled into the parking lot of a decent hotel, or at least it appeared decent from the outside. Levi parked his truck off to the right along the curb, leaving a spot next to his vehicle for Curt to park.

A deep moan escaped his lips as he almost tumbled out of his vehicle on numb legs. "God, I hate these long rides between venues."

"Yeah, me too. My ass is numb."

"Mine too. A bed will sure feel good." He glanced across the street, noticing a nice looking steak house not far. "Say, how about we get some dinner over there before we turn in. I'm starving."

Levi glanced in the direction he pointed. "Me too. That beef jerky I bought at the gas station didn't stay with me very long. Let's get a room first. They look like they are pretty full. I hope they have a room."

He followed Levi into the hotel lobby. It wasn't much to look at, but it was probably cheap. It looked clean though, which was good. He didn't do expensive on his budget these days. There was a large check-in desk to the left with two bored looking people standing behind it.

"Can we help you?"

"Yes, I need a room. Two double beds, please."

"Sorry. I only have one room left and it's a one queen."

Levi turned and looked at him with one eyebrow arched as if he was asking how they would manage in one bed. He smiled thinking this would be perfect. "I'm fine with it if you are."

"Okay. We'll take it."

After Levi got them situated with their room, they headed back for their vehicles to pull around the back of the hotel. He couldn't wait to get the rugged cowboy in bed with him later. He got hard just thinking about it.

Once Levi opened the door to their room, set his bag down on the bed and started to unload his stuff. He was an unpacker. He liked to have his things in the drawers, his shaving stuff on the vanity, his shampoo in the shower, and be at home even if it was for one night.

"Do you always unload everything when you stay in a hotel?"

"Yep."

"Wow. Okay."

"You don't?"

"No. I live out of my duffle except for personal things like shaving cream, razor, and shampoo."

"Well, the shower stall isn't huge, but there should be enough room for two."

Curt watched Levi's Adam's apple bob a couple of times as he swallowed. "Two?"

"You know. Two bottles of shampoo."

He almost laughed when Levi sighed. He could believe it was in disappointment, but he wasn't sure.

"Oh, yeah."

"Ready to eat?"

Levi swallowed again as his gaze traveled down Curt's frame. "Yeah, I'm starving too."

The look gave him the impression their thoughts might run along the same track after all. Tonight would be interesting to say the least.

Several minutes later, they were seated across from each other at the steak house. They'd each ordered a beer, a thick steak with all the fixings, and settled in to relax.

Curt toyed with the condensation on his beer bottle as he watched Levi across the table.

"What?"

"Nothing, why?"

"You're staring again."

"Sorry. Just trying to figure you out, is all."

"Nothing to figure out, really. I'm a simple guy. I like things easy. I ride bulls for a living. I want to retire from this crazy life pretty soon since I ain't gettin' any younger." He tipped the bottle of beer to his lips. "What about you?"

"I'm a pretty simple guy myself. I want to find someone to spend the rest of my life with at some point. You know, raise a family. That kind of thing."

"Oh?"

"Yeah. Maybe have a little place with some horses, cattle, kids, and dogs."

"You just need the white picket fence then and the little woman to keep your house clean."

Curt smiled knowing a little woman wasn't what he envisioned although a housekeeper would be great. He hated housework. "I would love someone to do the housework."

"Yeah, me too. That's one of those things that I hate doing. I'm a total slob when it comes to my bedroom. I don't even make my bed much." Levi took another sip before setting his beer back on the coaster. "Are you one of those people who puts everything in its place?"

"I like things put away, yeah, but I'm not a clean freak if that's what you mean."

"What about chores like mucking stalls?"

"I don't mind doing that. I love animals, so yeah, I'm good with doing chores around the home place. I have a horse at my parent's ranch and I take care of him when I'm home. They have the ranch hands watch him for me when I'm out on the road."

"How often do you get home?"

"Not enough. I try to get by there whenever we have a venue close enough to drive in between. That hasn't happened much the last couple of months though. These venues have been all over the fucking country. Back and forth from coast to coast makes it difficult to get home when you have to travel two days to get from one place to another."

"I know what you mean. The life is rough. I don't know how these guys do it with wives and kids."

Curt drained his beer. "Me either."

Their food arrived and as they both dug in to their thick, juicy steaks, conversation lagged. Thoughts were jumbled inside his head when he thought about lying in the same bed with Levi tonight. He almost groaned out loud when his cock began to get uncomfortable inside his jeans. He had to get laid soon or he would die of blue balls. "So, you up for a little fun tonight?"

Chapter Four

Levi wasn't sure he understood what Curt meant, but the grin on his partner's face spoke of something more than just drinking until they both couldn't walk back to the hotel. "Fun?"

"Yeah."

"What kind of fun are we talking about?" he asked, wondering if they were on the same page. Curt liked women, right? Didn't he take two to bed the night before?

Curt pushed his plate away and leaned back in the seat. Levi got the impression he was totally relaxed in his element. "If I'm totally off base here, let me know, but I get the distinct feeling you are into me."

Levi swallowed hard. *What the hell is he getting at?* "I'm not sure what you mean, Curt."

"I mean you want to fuck me."

Aw, hell. Levi blew out a breath, hesitating several seconds to gain the nerve to admit his sexual preference to the man across the table after keeping it a secret for so long. "Okay. Yes, I'm gay. I like men. I like you, but I get the feeling you are into women."

"I am."

"Then no worries. I won't try anything with you. I'm okay with it."

Curt leaned in toward the table. "Easy man. I'm bi."

"You're what?"

"Bi-sexual. I like both men and women depending on my moods. Today, I like men. Yesterday, I was into the two women in my room, but it ended up being a lady-fest so I watched. I got off on that too."

"Wow. All right then." Shock did a little dance down his spine. Curt did like men. Did he like him enough to want to fuck though? "So what exactly are you saying?"

"I want to be balls deep in your ass tonight," Curt whispered loud enough only he heard him. "Got a problem with that?"

Levi shivered in anticipation. "Nope."

"Good."

Levi wanted Curt's full lips wrapped around his cock more than anything in the world, but if he would actually have his fantasy man deep in his ass, he couldn't wait for the night to come.

After they paid their bills, they walked casually across the street to their hotel. Their steps grew rushed as they approached the door to their room. Levi pulled out the key card to open the door, but before he could slide it in, Curt grabbed him by the shoulder, spun him around and crushed his mouth against Levi's. Teeth gnashed, lips melded, and tongues danced as Curt pinned him to the door.

When Curt finally moved back, their breaths came out in ragged pants of desire and need.

"Let me open the door."

"Yeah."

Levi's hands shook as he tried to slide the key card into the lock. It took a couple of tries to get the card to work.

"Easy, cowboy. We got all night."

Levi glanced over his shoulder as he opened the door. "Anticipation is gonna kill me."

Curt gave him a crooked little smile that made his balls ache.

The door no more than banged shut before Curt was all over him, pulling at his clothes, unzipping his pants, and pushing both his shorts and jeans down.

"I want this cock."

"It's yours. Suck me."

Curt dropped to his knees in front of Levi. "I've wanted to suck this for months." Curt dove in, taking Levi's entire cock in his mouth. Levi wasn't necessarily a big man as far as cocks go, but having Curt deep throat him was enough to drive him up on his toes.

"Easy there," Curt whispered against his flesh as he licked his cock from base to tip. "Such a beautiful cock. You are one gorgeously endowed man."

"I want to see you."

"In a minute. I'm worshipping this magnificent piece of flesh here first. You'll get your chance." Curt sucked, licked, and swirled his tongue around and around Levi's cock.

Levi's leg shook from trying to hold back his orgasm. He need to come so bad, he felt like his head was about to explode out the end of his dick. "Please. I can't handle it anymore."

"Your turn, but first, in the shower," Curt said, getting to his feet as he began working the buttons on his shirt.

Within seconds, his clothes lay in a heap near Levi's shirt as he worked his boots and jeans off as well.

"I plan to fuck you clear into tomorrow."

Levi headed for the bathroom, hoping the shower was big enough for the both of them, but if not, they would have to migrate to the bed. He didn't care, either way. He leaned in to turn on the shower. Curt grabbed his hips, rubbing his hard cock along the crack of his ass.

"Are you ready for me?"

"Hell yeah. I've been ready for months."

"Me too."

"Why didn't you say something sooner?" Levi asked, turning to face him. "We could have been fucking already."

Curt kissed him lightly on the mouth. "I wasn't sure about you. I'd heard rumors, but nothing solid. You keep to yourself very well, so I had to make double sure before I approached you."

Once the door was open on the stall, they both stepped in under the spray of the hot water. Curt opened the soap and lathered his hands until they were slick. His hands were everywhere on Levi's body, smoothing over his chest, down between his legs, around to his ass, washing every inch of his body before he murmured, "Rinse."

Levi turned toward the water, letting it cascade over his face, neck, and chest as he felt Curt kneel in the shower stall and bite at his ass. He'd never felt anything so erotic in his life.

"Such a nice ass to fuck."

Curt spread his cheeks, kneading the twin globes in his hands as he licked and bit at the flesh of his butt. One finger rimmed his back hole, pushing in to the first knuckle. "You are tight, my friend."

"It's been a while."

"You're going to feel magnificent around my cock." Levi clenched his ass around Curt's finger. "Oh yeah. You like the sound of that, don't you?"

"Fuck."

"We will do that too."

Levi closed his eyes as he pushed back against Curt's fingers. He thought back, realizing it had been several months since he'd had sex, and man, was he primed to go off in seconds after Curt penetrated his ass. He wouldn't be able to hold back for very long even though he wanted to ream Curt's ass, too, before the night was over.

"Wash me," Curt said, standing behind him.

Levi grabbed the soap, turned around and lathered up Curt's body. He loved the feel of hard chest under his hands. The muscles bunched and rolled with his touch, giving away the fact that Curt wasn't immune to his touch either. Curt's cock strained upward from the nest of curls at the base. Balls heavy with cum hung low. His shaft was long and thick with a cut head and what was this? Curt wore a Prince Albert piercing.

"You're pierced."

"Yeah. From what I understand, it feels awesome raking the walls of your ass. You should get one."

"Yeah, no. No one is coming near me with a needle. I don't do tats or piercings, but this looks wicked. I can't wait to feel it."

Curt rinsed the soap from his body before he demanded, "Suck me, right now."

Levi kneeled in front of Curt, massaging his length with his hand. "You're very well endowed."

"I'm glad you approve. I want your mouth."

Levi hummed his approval as he took the head of Curt's dick between his lips, flicking the piercing with his tongue. The little ring slid along his tongue as he took more of Curt's cock in his mouth, sucking hard on the flesh. Curt took Levi's hair in his fists, guiding him up and down the hard length just like he wanted it.

After several minutes, Curt pulled loose of Levi's mouth. "Nice, but I want your ass when I come."

They shut the water off before towel drying each other and then heading into the other room. Levi took a seat on the bed. "I'm so ready for you, I can hardly sit still."

"On your stomach. Spread your legs. I'll get the lube and condoms."

As Levi rolled over, he heard the drawer of the dresser open and close. Cool, slick gel coated his ass seconds later.

The crinkle of a condom wrapper brought his attention back to the task at hand, spreading his legs and relaxing his hole. He knew this first time would be something to remember, especially since he wasn't sure if there would be a second time or third.

The heavy head of Curt's cock bumped against his ass as he pushed out the breath he wasn't aware he'd been holding. "Relax and hold your ass open for me."

Levi spread the cheeks of his ass before Curt pushed past the ring of muscles with a slight pop.

"I'm in."

"Fuck yeah."

"Wow, you are tight." Curt pushed in a little farther. "You okay?"

"Yeah." He shivered as Curt's piercing raked along his anal walls. "Oh my God. That piercing is amazing."

"Told you." Curt pushed until he was balls deep. "You feel amazing."

"You're pretty amazing yourself. Can you move please? I'm dying here. I need to come so bad, I hurt."

Curt began to move, the thrust of his hips keeping perfectly rhythm with the ticking of the old fashioned clock on the bedside table. The burn of having Curt's cock in his ass, the perfect, sweet pain he longed for having come full circle. The stretch was incredible.

Thrusts became uncoordinated as Curt moaned behind him. Levi's balls burned. The ache drove him out of his mind with lust.

Curt reached around, fisting Levi's cock in his hand as he pumped several times. "Come for me, Levi. I want to feel your cum on my hand. I want you to squirt your satisfaction all over this bed."

Levi lost what little control he had over his desire as he exploded in a shout of satisfaction loud enough the entire complex of rooms probably heard him.

Curt continued to pump with his hand and his hips until he too, shouted his release in a cry of fulfillment.

The weight of the other man against his back as they both relaxed onto the bed felt wonderful.

"I need to get rid of this condom, but I'm exhausted now."

"Me too."

"I'm not done with you by a long shot, so I hope you are up for more in say an hour?"

"If you are ready for me to ride you, sure." Levi felt the smile on his skin.

"You bet."

The slide of Curt's cock from his ass made him groan. The loss of the touch of his hands, left him feeling empty. He wanted more, definitely more.

Curt disappeared into the bathroom as Levi stayed on the bed with his arms out, his legs spread, and his ass sore. He loved it.

Water ran for several minutes as he assumed Curt was disposing of the condom and washing up. He'd have to move in a minute, he figured, to clean himself up. Although, he wasn't sure how any intimacy was going to work between them. The after sex thing always mystified him. He thought of Curt as a friend. How would things be between them now, he wasn't sure, but he wanted the explosive sex to continue for a while. They would have to keep their relationship, whatever it was, on the down low on the circuit. Coming out around others as fuck buddies would make things a bit awkward, to say the least.

A blow landed on his right ass cheek.

He jumped and flipped over onto his back, his stinging butt on fire. "Fuck! That hurt."

Curt laughed. "Get your ass up. I'll be ready for more shortly and this time I want to feel your cock in me."

"I can barely move and you're ready for round two?" Levi asked, his body beginning to like the idea of more.

"Hell yeah, but if you need a little more time to recuperate, I'm okay with that. I'll sit here and stroke myself until you're ready." Curt sat at the top of the bed against the headboard, his cock flaccid at the moment, but as he started to stroke his shaft, it began to get hard again.

I'm going to die a happy man.

Levi got to his feet and headed into the bathroom to wash up a bit. The lube on his ass and between his legs felt sticky. He needed to wipe the stuff off before they went at it again. "How do you like it?"

"What do you mean?"

"Do you want me to build you up first or drive right in with a heavy plunge?"

"I want you to fuck me hard. It's been quite a while since I've been with another man. I've been banging the women lately."

"How long has it been?"

"Six months or so."

"You'll be tight then too."

"Yeah probably."

Levi poked his head around the corner. Curt was at full arousal. "I really liked that piercing. That was interesting to say the least."

"I thought you might like it."

"I've never been with anyone that had one, so yeah, it was hot."

"Good."

Curt's cock bobbed against his stomach. The man had a healthy girth and length. It was no wonder Levi's ass still stung from his penetration. Even then, he couldn't wait to be fucked again. Levi returned to the vanity, took out a wash cloth, rubbed some soap on it, and scrubbed his ass and balls. One thing he always liked when he went down on a man was a freshly washed groin. The smell of soap on the skin did something for him in the way of arousal. He got off on the scent.

After he dried off, he walked back toward the bed. Curt still slowly stroked his cock as he watched Levi move around the bottom and to the other side. Levi slid onto the bed before burying his face in Curt's groin. "You smell good."

"Suck me."

"My pleasure." Levi flicked the piercing with his tongue, hoping it would drive Curt insane with need as the vibration zipped down his cock. He licked from balls to tip in one long stroke before taking the head into his mouth. Quick sucking motions right on the head had Curt's hips coming up off the bed to force him to take more into his mouth.

"More."

Levi sucks the head into his mouth, but didn't go down any farther. He wanted to drive the younger man insane with need. Slow strokes of his fingers around Curt's balls, brought a moan from him. His breath came out in short pants as the moans became louder.

"Fuck yeah."

When Levi penetrated his ass with one finger, Curt surged upward, shoving his cock clear to the back of Levi's throat. Forcing his breath out through his nose, he sucked and finger fucked Curt until the other man shot cum out the end of his dick in long, stringy spurts.

"Oh God," Curt moaned as he fisted Levi's head, quickly fucking his mouth until the hot cum ceased. "That was fantastic, but I still want you in my ass."

"I plan to fuck you hard enough to make you come again."

"We'll see about that. Three times inside of a couple of hours might be a bit much, but you can do your best." Curt scooted down on the bed so his head was on the pillow. "How do you want me? This is your show."

"Uh, just like that is good. Spread your legs and pull them up near your head." Curt complied, opening his ass for Levi. "Perfect." Levi grabbed a condom, and the tube of lube. He liberally spread some of the silky liquid around Curt's ass, pushed some in through the ring of muscles to lubricate his way. "Ready?"

"Hell yeah."

Levi positioned himself between Curt's legs as the other man pulled his knees to his chest. Taking his cock in hand, he slipped the condom over his length, and then began the slow fucking of the man beneath him.

When he managed to push himself past the ring of muscles in Curt's ass, he sighed at the feeling. The tightness almost brought his balls up in an explosive orgasm much too soon. He beat it down with sheer force of will. He didn't want to come quite yet. He wanted to enjoy the silky slide of his cock through the tunnel of Curt's ass for several minutes longer before he gave into his own need.

Levi looked down to where their bodies met, loving the sight. Being buried in Curt's backside was heaven on earth. As he slowly began to thrust his hips, Curt moaned and closed his eyes.

"Harder."

"Nope. My way this time."

"Fuck. You're gonna kill me."

Levi smiled. He kind of liked having the other man under his control. He wasn't the alpha type male most of the time, but this, this was way better than anything he'd ever felt before. He moved slowly, painstakingly slow as he fucked Curt.

Soon, he couldn't handle the deliberately measured glide of his cock. He needed more. He needed faster. He needed to fuck Curt like there would be no tomorrow for them. Maybe there would, maybe there wouldn't. At this point he didn't know.

With a hard thrust of his hips, he buried his cock balls deep.

"That's it. Hard. Oh God, harder."

Levi jammed his cock into Curt's ass so hard, he felt the other man hit his head on the headboard of the bed. Levi grabbed the edge of the decorative piece of furniture, to give him more leverage. "I'm going to fuck you so hard, you'll come again. Come for me, Curt."

"Yes!"

Cum spurted out of the end of his cock, painting his abdomen in white, long lines, just as Levi felt his own orgasm give way, pushing cum to the end of the condom in a rush of adrenaline almost like they got bull riding. Levi shouted with his own release.

Levi's body shook with such force he didn't think he'd ever come so hard in his life as he had fucking Curt. He held himself up by sheer will as his cock softened inside Curt's ass.

"You're pretty good at that. I don't think I've come so hard in my life and you managed to get me off three times tonight. That has to be a record for me."

Levi grinned as he slowly withdrew his cock. He slipped off and tied the end of the condom to dispose of it in the trashcan the moment he could feel his legs again or had the strength to move.

Curt got up from the bed and went to wash off. "I'm going to take another shower real quick to get this off. Want to join me?"

"I think I'd better not."

"Aw, tired, old man?"

Levi jumped from the bed with more energy than he thought he possessed, and smacked Curt on the ass. "Don't get sassy with me."

Spinning around, Curt yanked him close enough their cocks rubbed together. "I like your hand on my ass, your cock in my ass, your mouth on my cock, and you fucking me so hard, we bang headboards, but don't think you run this relationship. I'm in charge." He nipped at Levi's mouth. "Say it. Who's in charge?"

"You."

"Good." He growled as he crushed their mouths together. When they finally came up for air, Curt said, "Now, I'll be back in a minute."

Curt disappeared through the door to the shower, leaving Levi to ponder what the hell he'd gotten himself into.

Chapter Five

When Levi awoke the next morning, he was curled into Curt's side with his head on the man's chest. He'd never slept this hard before, but he certainly had the night before. Coming twice might have been the culprit for his good night sleep. He wasn't going to complain, especially when they had another twelve hours on the road today before they made Oklahoma City.

"Mornin'," Curt said with a sleepy growl to his voice. "How'd you sleep?"

"Good," Levi answered, pushing himself up and off the side of the bed. Grabbing his jeans from the floor, he slipped them up and over his hips before heading into the bathroom to take a leak.

"We should get some breakfast before we head out, that way we won't have to stop for several hours."

"Good idea." Levi came back into the room and found Curt already up with his jeans on. Disappointed at not seeing the other man in his full naked glory, he sighed and grabbed for some clean clothes. "I'm going to shower real quick."

"Sounds good. I need to check my voicemail and email this morning, so I'll see you in a bit."

The disappointment compounded before Levi hit the shower. He'd hoped Curt would join him for a quick romp before they headed out, but apparently the other man wasn't in the mood this morning.

As Levi scrubbed his head, letting the shampoo sluice down his chest, he thought about last night. He and Curt were very compatible in bed together, but how would the whole bi thing work if they were going to be fuck buddies? Levi really didn't do women. What if Curt wanted to go out and fuck a lady every once in a while without Levi? Did Levi want to share what he'd found with Curt? What would happen when they got back around the other guys on the circuit? What exactly had they found together anyway?

All of these things rushed through his brain at lightning speed as he washed his body. *No use over thinking things right now. Curt is in charge so I guess I'll sit back and see what happens in the future. I can't get too tied up with him if I want to keep things simple.*

After he finished his shower, he toweled off, pulled on his clean underwear and jeans before slipping on his T-shirt. He padded back out to dump his dirty jeans in his duffle as he overheard Curt on the phone.

"No. I'm done with this."

Levi listened closely in hopes he might be able to help his friend.

"I can't help you again. You need to stand on your own two feet, Missy. I can't keep giving you money for you to waste it on whatever you are using it for beyond your rent and living expenses."

Silence.

Curt pushed his hand through his hair.

Levi wanted to smooth it back into place.

"Fine. I'll send you five hundred, but no more. I have to worry about my own future and you are killing me here. I'm only helping because of the kids, you know that, right? They are the most important thing."

Kids

"I'll stop somewhere on my way to Oklahoma and wire it to you. It's the best I can do."

Levi felt bad for eavesdropping. He shouldn't be listening. Curt's life was his own and none of Levi's business, but he couldn't help but hear what was being said.

"I love you too. Please, buy groceries with this." Curt turned and noticed Levi standing there. "All right. I have to go. Talk to you soon. Bye."

Curt pushed the button on the phone before tossing it on the bed. "Sorry about that."

"Nothing to be sorry for." Levi pulled on clean socks and his boots. "Do you want to talk about it?"

"No."

"Okay."

They silently grabbed their gear before heading out to their respective vehicles.

"Listen, Levi. I'm sorry, but it's a family thing and I don't want to drag you into it. I'll handle it."

"No problem."

"Shall we stop at the Dunkin' Donuts over there for something to eat before we hit the road?"

"Sounds good."

They got into their trucks, started them up and drove across the road for food. Neither spoke during their short breakfast until they were done and moving back toward their vehicles again.

"Signal me when you're ready to stop for gas, leak stop or whatever."

"Sure, Curt."

Levi climbed into his truck cab and slammed the door. He didn't know what to make of Curt's distance this morning after their romping night of sex. Was it a one-night stand they'd had and it was over now? *Shit. This totally sucks.*

Twelve hours, twelve fucking hours in the truck until he saw the Oklahoma City limits. He couldn't have been happier even though he didn't know what the night would bring or the coming days. He just wanted to get the hell out of his truck for the night. His shoulder wasn't bad considering what they'd done the night before, but it had stiffened up some with the long ride.

Curt had been distant all day. Every time they had stopped, he wouldn't say much whether it be for gas, food or a leak. Well, he wasn't in the mood to fuck around either. He just wanted to get some sleep, find out where they needed to check in for the venue in a couple of days, find some food, and chill out, not especially in any order. "Where do you want to eat?"

"I don't care. I just want food, a bed, a beer, and sleep."

"Me too." They found a burger place close to the hotel where the riders would stay, ordered some takeout, then headed back to the hotel. "You can stay here for the few days it will be before the other riders start coming in. Tomorrow, I'm going to head home."

"Home as in your ranch?"

"Yeah, it's only a little over an hour from here."

"Why didn't you say so? We could have gone there instead of staying here tonight."

"I would have, but I didn't think you'd want to hang at my place until the rides start."

"Sure I would. It would be like being home for me, Levi. I think it would be great to see your place."

Levi sat on the bed as they ate their food. "All right. Tomorrow morning we'll head over there. We have three days until this weekend's rides begin. We can get on some practice bulls if you want, ride some horses, do some chores, and whatever else you want to do."

"Sounds like a plan," Curt replied, stuffing a French fry in his mouth. "I didn't realize you lived this close."

"Yeah, this is one of the venues I used to come to when I wasn't riding, to watch the guys on the bulls. It was a real rush for me. I tried to be down as close as possible to the dirt. I wanted to smell the sweat on the bull, let the dirt cloud settle on my skin, and hang with the riders. I made friends with a lot of the guys before I ever got on the circuit. I learned a lot from these guys." Levi finished his burger, stuffed the wrapper back in the bag, and then leaned back on his elbows on the bed.

"I bet."

"How did you start?"

"Doing the small rodeos, riding some when I could, you know. I had a good teacher. One of the retired guys, Clay Richie, took me under his wing."

"You rode with Clay Richie?" he asked, sitting straight up.

Curt shrugged as he waded up the wrapper of his burger. "Yeah. I spent several summers on his place doing chores while he taught me how to ride bulls."

"Wow. He's a legend."

"I know, and a good friend."

"Do you see him much anymore?"

"When I can. He lives not far from my parent's place outside Amarillo. He has a riding school for guys who want to learn how and does very well at it, from what I understand."

Levi leaned forward, dangling his hands between his knees. "Great start. You seem like a natural on the back of a bull."

"Thanks. That means a lot coming from you."

"Why me?"

"You've been around a long time, Levi. Your tips are great for guys to learn. It helps to get out of your head when you're about to go for the ride of your life for eight seconds. You know, we all get too wound up in our heads some times."

"I know. I do it too."

Curt got up and started putting his stuff in the drawers of the dresser. Levi figured it was an automatic thing for him that he did without even realizing he was doing it.

"Yeah, but you've learned how to get out of your head before you ride. Some guys can't do that and it makes it hard to stay on the back of a two-thousand pound animal who doesn't want you there."

"Guys need to learn how to separate their lives from their riding."

"True, and you seem to be one of the best at it. They learn by example. You're a great model for that way of thinking."

"I'm just a man who has been on a lot of bulls. I had a hard time learning that lesson too, but something clicked in my head several years ago. You could probably tell by how my career went after it did. My riding got better, my scores got better, and I started to win. I'm on the verge of qualifying for my sixth finals with a shot at the world title. Everyone is so close in numbers that's it anyone's game."

"I'll have to try that. I tend to over think things before they open the chute."

"I know. I can tell when you do. If you clear your mind, when that gate opens you'll be so focused on staying your ass on the bull, you won't have time to think, just react. Let your body compensate for the bulls movement and you'll ride better."

"Thanks."

"No problem."

"Wanna fuck?" Curt asked, startling Levi with the question.

"Seriously?"

"Hell yeah. I want more of what we had last night."

"I wasn't sure there would be more with your mood today."

"Sorry. It didn't have anything to do with you, it's family business."

"You can talk to me if you want."

"No. It's fine. Nothing you need to worry about." When Curt stood, his hands went to his belt. "So are you up or down?"

Levi shivered as desire rolled through him. He wanted Curt's dick in his ass more than anything right this moment. "Up."

With his pants down around his boots, Curt looked like something out of a wet dream. Levi thought it was sexy as hell that Curt went commando. His dick curved slightly to the left when he was full erect, like now. Levi's mouth watered to taste. He wanted to feel that piercing on his tongue. He wanted to lick that little pearl of pre-cum resting on the end of Curt's cock.

"You want to taste me?"

"Hell yeah."

"Come and get it."

Levi slid to his knees on the floor in front of Curt, taking his cock in hand and stroking it several times before he enveloped his cockhead in his mouth. Saliva filled his mouth as he went down and back up, slicking up the skin. He let his fingers play with the knobs hanging low between Curt's legs.

Curt groaned, fisting Levi's hair in his hands. He loved the feel of Curt losing his hold on his sanity while Levi made him feel good.

"You are really good at this."

He let his tongue slide up Curt's cock. "I try. I happen to enjoy sucking you off."

"Just me?"

"Just you."

Curt's hips pushed forward. The piercing raked along Levi's tongue as he sucked as much of Curt's cock into his mouth as he could. He loved the feel of the other man in his mouth.

"Enough," Curt growled, pulling his cock from between Levi's lips. "I want your ass. Now." Curt toed off his boots and socks before shucking his jeans and pulling off his shirt.

Levi stood, pushing his jeans to the floor before ripping his T-shirt over his head. He sat on the bed to remove his socks and boots, but Curt's mouth took up residence around his cock for a moment. "So good."

"You taste fantastic. I'd make you come with my mouth, but I can't wait to feel your ass squeeze me so tight, I almost lose it."

Curt moved back on his haunches to let Levi remove the rest of his clothes. "On the bed. Legs up to your chest. Spread that asshole for me." Curt disappeared for a moment as Levi positioned himself on the bed.

He felt the squirt of lube on his crack seconds later. "Hurry."

The rigid head of Curt's cock bumped at his back hole and slowly penetrated through the ring of muscles guarding his anus.

Sweet mother of God.

The burn felt like heaven and hell at the same time. If he hadn't remembered the sex vividly from the night before, he would have sworn they'd never done this before, but there it was. The stretch, the sting, and then the pleasure. "Fuck me hard. God, please hard." Curt slammed his pelvis against Levi's ass as he pushed his dick all the way inside. He felt so full, so stretched.

Curt grabbed his legs near the knees, holding him still while he pounded into him with an increasingly erratic rhythm. Levi's orgasm was close, so close. He felt his balls draw up.

"Come for me, Levi. I want to feel your ass milk my cock."

"Ah!" Levi exploded in an orgasm so heavy, he almost blacked out as cum shot up his abdomen, the white streaks painting his skin in long, thin lines. He moaned as Curt continued to pound into him for several more long seconds before he too lost the control he had on his pleasure.

"Fuck yeah."

Breathing became a premium as his racing heart pounded against his chest wall. Curt panted heavily too as they slowly came down from their orgasmic high.

"You are amazing," Curt whispered as he leaned in, kissing Levi on the mouth.

"Thanks. You're pretty great yourself." Curt's cock slid out of his ass, allowing Levi to slowly lower his legs until his feet were planted on the floor. "I need a shower."

"Mind if I join you?"

"Not at all. I would love for you to wash my back," he said as he stood. Curt landed a smack to his left ass cheek.

"Naughty boy."

After a nice, hot shower with some additional raunchy sex, they decided to get a beer at the local honkytonk a few blocks down from the hotel. It would probably be where the riders would hang out after the show on Friday and Saturday before they left for the next stop in South Dakota.

The bar looked quaint with its old western feel. The tables weren't too full since it was a Tuesday night, so they found one in the corner, ordered a couple of beers and settled in. Levi wanted to unwind after the long drive.

Here they might be able to scope things out, tease each other a little before going back to the hotel. It wasn't a gay bar though, which left them staying away from each other for the most part. He might be able to stroke Curt under the table without too many people noticing though. With it being your typical western bar, most of the couples were men and women. The sea of cowboy hats, rhinestone pockets on the backs of jeans, cowboy boots, and belt buckles reminded him of a Texas bar he'd went to once. He'd almost been in a fight that night as he tried to pick up a guy he thought was gay. Turned out he wasn't. Levi ended up with a bloody nose and a black eye. He'd been a lot more careful since.

"How are things at home with you being gay? Do your parents support you?"

"Oh yeah. They just want me to find a nice person to settle down with." He tipped the bottle of beer to his lips. "What about you? How does your family take your sexual preferences?"

"They don't know about me being bi. They know about the women, of course, but not the men."

"That must be hard."

"It is. My mom is really pushing for me to find a nice girl and settle down, but I'm not sure if I want a wife or not."

"How often do you do women?"

"It depends on how I'm feeling. The last six months, there have been a lot of women, mostly buckle bunnies, of course. We have to be careful around the circuit."

"Don't I know it."

"Is that why I didn't see you much in the bars where the guys hang out?"

"Yep. I would tend to find a gay bar in the town we were visiting, lose the cowboy persona and try to find someone to hook up with. It worked some times, other times not."

"Have you ever been with a woman?"

"Yeah. Twice. It wasn't a pleasant experience. Not that I found the women lacking, I just didn't get as worked up with women as I do with men. I prefer my own kind, I guess."

"I have a hankering for a woman now and again, but for the most part, I prefer men. The sex is more along the lines of what turns me on, rough and pleasurable."

Levi drained his beer and signaled the waitress for another round. "Just the way I like it too."

"We are very compatible, you and I." Curt swirled the beer around in his bottle before finishing off the remainder of his own drink.

"I think so." Levi leaned his elbows on the table. "I think you'll like my place."

"How many acres did you say you had?"

"Five-hundred."

Curt whistled in appreciation. "My dream place is to have a nice little ranch house with some acreage where I can raise animals."

The waitress brought their beers and as Levi paid her, he said, "I want to get a few bulls into the ranks of the circuit. I think it would be great, although I would be gone all the time still." He shrugged. "Maybe I'll just stick to training cutting horses."

"Whatever you want to do, I'm sure you'll be great at it. Maybe you should train riders like Clay does."

"Maybe." Levi contemplated the brown bottle in his hands.

Music blared over the speakers from the DJ at the front of the bar. They apparently didn't have a band on a Tuesday night. No worries. The DJ was doing a pretty good job playing the latest country tunes out there. Several people were dancing, which was always a good sign. Lights swirled around the dance floor, reflecting off the sparkling rhinestones on the women's clothing. Men were decked out in their Saturday night finery with button down shirts, pressed jeans, and brushed clean boots. He wondered how many of them were real cowboys and how many of them were wannabes.

The cowboys hanging around the bar looked nice. Round asses in their Wrangler jeans, tempted him beyond temptation. He wouldn't act on the temptation though. He had Curt, at least for now, and he wasn't one to step out on someone he was with even if they weren't a couple. Come to think of it, he wasn't sure what they were. Playing it by ear seemed like a good plan though. He might be able to find out more about how Curt wanted this to go while they were at his ranch chilling out.

"What time do you want to leave in the morning for your place?"

"Probably around nine or whenever we get up. I'm not in any rush. Morning chores will have already been done by the time we get there anyway. Six a.m. comes pretty early on a working ranch."

"Yes it does."

"I have plenty of room at the house. It's four bedrooms, three bathrooms. You can have you own room while you're there."

"We won't be sleeping together?"

"Well, I wasn't sure how you wanted to proceed while we are there. My ranch hands know I'm gay and they are okay with it. In fact, several of my guys are gay too. The barn gets a lot of use."

Curt laughed as he tipped his head back on his shoulders. When their gazes met again, Levi could see the smirk on his lips and the amusement in his eyes. "Why am I not surprised. You seemed to have quite the set up there."

He nodded. "Yeah, I guess I do. It's pretty sweet actually."

"Did you do your ranch hands?" Curt asked, before taking a sip of his beer like he didn't just drop a bombshell.

Levi wasn't sure how to answer that. He had…once, and it was the worst mistake of his life. "No. I figured I needed to keep the boss/employee thing separate."

"Have you ever had a serious relationship?"

"Yeah, once. He was a local cowboy who came out to the ranch one day looking for work. I hired him. Thus the reason I don't do the ranch hands anymore. Things didn't end well when he took off the parts unknown after killing me financially."

"He stole from you?"

Levi sipped his beer, while he contemplated how much to tell Curt. It was a difficult time in his life and one he didn't want to relive, but he figured since Curt asked, maybe he might have a little more in mind for them than just fuck buddies. "In a sense, yes. I gave him everything. He had access to all my financial information, ranch books, credit cards, the works. He took me for ten thousand dollars and disappeared after he cleaned out my bank account, ran up my cards, and fucked up my books."

"You sound bitter."

"I am."

"Do you still have feelings for him?" Curt asked, his gaze narrowing as he searched Levi's face for the answer.

With a shake of his head, he said, "No. I'm more pissed that I was so gullible to start with, than anything. I should have seen it coming, but I thought I was in love." He drained his beer. "I won't be so easy to dupe again."

"I can imagine."

"Have you ever been in love?"

Chapter Six

"No, can't say that I have. I'm not even sure I would know what it felt like, although I have an idea."

"What would it feel like to you?"

"Wanting to be with that person, twenty-four seven, needing to please them with every breath, taking their every want, need, and desire into consideration with every move I make, not worrying about what other people say when it comes to that person." He shrugged. "I guess that's my take on the matter."

"Sounds like you have it down pretty well."

"Maybe, although I'm not sure if I would recognize it in time to act on it. I haven't felt that way about anyone, yet, even though my family is all about me settling down and leaving the circuit. I'm not ready for that yet."

"You're a good rider. You should ride for a while yet, unless you get hurt."

"If I don't make finals this year, I'm going to need to reevaluate my career choice, I think."

"Why?"

"Because I haven't made finals since I started five years ago. I should have been able to get in the first year."

"That's pretty aggressive to think you'll make finals that quickly."

"It's what I thought." Curt peeled the paper off his bottle before stacking it to his left with the last one. "Being that good was what came naturally to me or so it seemed, but when you're riding in the big leagues, you're just another rider trying to make it. You aren't anyone. I was on top of the world in the smaller venues. I won almost every event, but here, it isn't so easy. These guys are good, the best, and they take no prisoners."

"True. It's a rough business to be in, that's why you have to think about after you retire. What are you going to do to make a living? You can't ride bulls forever. Most guys don't make it past thirty-five as a bull rider and I'm pushing thirty-three now."

"You are five years older than me then."

Levi smiled. He'd pegged Curt to be in his mid-twenties a long time ago so it wasn't news to him to know the younger man was twenty-eight. "You're just a youngin'."

"Yeah, whatever, old man."

They laughed together for a moment. "No, seriously. What are your plans for after you are done bull riding?"

"I'm not sure. I might go back to school for a business degree. I started out doing that before I came on the circuit full time while I was training with Clay. I'm only a few classes short of my bachelor's degree in business."

"Sounds good."

"I really need a master's though to do much with it. That would take another couple of years, but I would be able to be in a good position with a company as a vice president or something or help someone run their business who is struggling to make it financially profitable."

"Do you know accounting?"

"Yep. Numbers are my specialty."

"Maybe I'll have you take a look at my books when we get the ranch. I need some help with that."

"Sure." He grinned as he cocked one eyebrow up over his left eye. "I won't even charge you…much."

I kind of like the sound of those terms. "Much?"

"Yeah. A little ass reaming is in order, I would think."

Levi reached under the table to take Curt's dick in his hand. The man was already hard behind the fly of his jeans. Levi stroked the rigid flesh a few times for good measure before removing his hand.

"What the fuck? We got us a couple of queers here, gentlemen!" One big, burly cowboy stood near the edge of the table. "We don't take kindly to your type in our bar."

"We are drinking our beers, man. Leave us be."

A crowd began to gather behind him. "We like our women hot, our beer cold, and our bar free of queers. Get the fuck out."

"We aren't hurting anyone by sitting here drinking our beer."

The guy swept the table free of beer bottles, spilling what was left of their beers on the floor. "You're done. Leave now before I throw your asses out in the street after I beat you both to a pulp."

Curt slowly climbed to his feet. "That so?"

"Yeah, that's so." The guy went to grab Curt by the front of his shirt.

Curt pulled back his massive arm, punching the guy square in the nose.

"You fucker! You broke my nose." The guy lunged, taking them both to the floor. Blood smeared across Curt's cheek as the other guy landed on top of him.

Bouncers appeared, dragging the two men apart. "Out. Both of you."

"We weren't doing anything but sitting here enjoying our beer," Levi said as the bouncers held the two men a big enough distance apart, they couldn't hit each other again.

"Who threw the first punch?"

The crowd pointed at Curt. "I did."

"Well, since he jumped you after that, you both need to vacate the premises. Your night is over."

Levi moved toward the door figuring Curt would follow as soon as the bouncer let him go.

"Fucking queers!" the guy shouted from behind them as the crowd parted to allow them through to the door.

The door stood between him and the outside fresh air. He hated it, but people just didn't understand. With that kind of man, how could they? He obviously had a problem with gay people, but it was his problem, not theirs. The guy seemed to be the typical downhome country boy who didn't like anything that wasn't the norm. He probably had a thing for anyone who wasn't white and female. Oh well, his problem.

"Hey, queer!" Great. The guy had followed them outside. "Hey, I'm talking to you."

Levi and Curt kept going. The guy appeared near Levi's truck with a baseball bat. With one swing, he took out Levi's right front headlight.

"I'm going to kill him," Curt said, coming back around the front of the truck as Levi tried to stop it.

"It's not worth it."

"He busted out your headlight!" Curt surged forward, grabbing the bat in mid-swing as the guy prepared to take out the other headlight. "You fucking moron. You have no idea how diminished your brain capacity is, do you?"

"What did you say?"

"I said you are a fucking moron. Come on. Swing at me, asshole."

The bat whizzed by Curt's head as he ducked. His fist connected with the guy's middle, pushing air out in a whoosh. The guy doubled over. Curt's foot came up between the man's legs, crushing his dick in one swift blow. He dropped the bat, grabbed his crotch, and fell on the ground moaning.

"Let's get out of here before the cops show up," Curt said, grabbing the doorknob to Levi's truck.

Levi jumped into the driver's seat, slammed the door, and cranked the truck over as a group of men came out of the bar. Gravel flew as they peeled out of the bar parking lot. "You okay?" he asked, worried Curt had been hurt in the fight.

"I'm good. The guy didn't even hit me."

He glanced across the cab of the truck, giving Curt a once over to make sure he wasn't bleeding anywhere or anything. "You're a pretty good fighter."

"I had to be in school. I was the skinny, little dude with the glasses."

"You were?"

"Yep."

"You'd better wash that blood off when we get back. No telling where that guy has been."

"I will."

They pulled back through the parking lot of the hotel. "Thanks for taking care of him."

"No problem."

"I'm not much of a fighter. I tend to avoid things like that if possible."

"He was completely out of line."

"Well, we weren't in a bar that catered to our kind."

They met around the front of the truck.

"Our kind?"

"You know, gay guys or girls."

"We're free to hang out anywhere we want."

"I know, but we're better staying with a bar where it's okay to be gay."

"I like country bars."

"So do I, but those types of patrons aren't okay with us touching, dancing, kissing or whatever. If we went to a gay bar, it would be the norm."

Curt leaned in to get nose-to-nose with Levi. "There is nothing wrong with being gay, Levi. We aren't sick or crazy. We happen to have a sexual preference for someone of the same sex. We are hardwired differently, more than likely from birth, although nothing has been proven one way or another. I, for one, am not ashamed to say I like you, I want to fuck you, and I plan for this to be a nice relationship whether it be for a long time or a short time. That all depends on you." Curt crushed their mouths together in a bruising kiss meant to bend his will to the more dominant man in this relationship.

When they finally came up for air, they were both breathing hard.

"You need to learn to embrace your sexuality and not let others tell you you're wrong because of your sexual preferences."

"I can't help the type of person I want to have sex with happens to be another man."

"No you can't, but stop being sorry for it. There isn't anything you can to do change it." Curt pressed his forehead against Levi's. "We should probably take this upstairs before I end up fucking you out here in the middle of the grass where everyone can see. I'm not so much into exhibitionism, but I might be able to get into that with you."

"Are you going to fuck me?"

"Hard and fast, buddy, hard and fast."

Levi almost ran up the stairs to their room, his shaking hands making it hard to slip the keycard in the door.

"Let me," Curt said, taking the card from him.

The door no more than banged shut behind them before Curt spun him around, yanked his T-shirt over his head and crushed their mouths together again. Levi loved it when Curt took control of their lovemaking and he had a feeling this time would be without much preamble at all. Like he said, hard and fast. Levi's cock hurt from being so turned on by the commanding attitude Curt had taken with him. He never knew he liked to be the weaker of the couple, but this made him realize he did. He wanted to be the more submissive of the two of them.

"Strip those jeans off while I get the lube and the condom."

Curt watched as Levi slowly unbuckled his belt buckle, the clanking noise loud in the quiet room. He unbuttoned his pants and hooked his fingers into the waistband of the jeans, before pushing them to the floor with his boxers. He sat on the side of the bed to toe off his boots and remove his socks before discarding his jeans in quick order.

A condom and the tube of lube were clutched in Curt's fist as he licked his lips. "You are so fucking hot."

"You are pretty scorching yourself." Levi wiped his sweaty palms on his thighs as he waited for Curt to undress. "Are you going to strip those jeans off or fuck me with them on?"

"I'm going to fuck you with them around my knees, because I'm so horny right now, my balls feel like they're about to explode from the sheer force of my cum building up inside them."

Levi rolled over on the bed, brought his knees up on the edge of the bed and spread his ass cheeks. "Do it." The cold drizzle of lube down the crack of his ass sent shivers racing down his spine. The hard head of Curt's cock bumped against the puckered hole of his ass. When Curt pushed through the ring of muscles and in until he was fully seated, Levi had to exhale sharply as the burn of sweet pain almost overwhelmed him.

"God, you feel amazing."

"Fuck me hard."

Curt withdrew his cock before shoving it back in with enough force to push Levi down on the bed. The hard thrusting of his hips felt fantastic. Levi wanted this round to go on and on, but soon it would be over and they would have to face their growing attraction for each other, at least Levi thought so.

* * * *

The tight ass of the man beneath him had Curt groaning his own satisfaction. He loved having Levi under him, in him, around him, sucking him, and fucking him. What he didn't like was how Levi shied away from embracing his sexual preference as normal. There wasn't anything abnormal about them being attracted to one another. He would have to work on that with his friend and lover.

Right now, he had an ass to plunder.

Levi braced himself for Curt's penetration, pushing back against Curt's hard thrust. He wasn't one to normally take someone so forcibly or so hard, but he needed this, wanted this, and craved it with Levi more than anything to date. The thought of Levi fucking anyone else like this drove him past crazy onto possessive. He wouldn't let go of his fuck buddy so easily. They would have to figure out how to make this work on the circuit without letting everyone else in on their extracurricular activities, after all it was no one's business what they did in their room, right?

Curt rammed his cock in several more times before he let his own climax overtake him. Levi hadn't come. Good. He was about to find out what it was like to be controlled.

When Curt removed his cock, Levi moaned. The disappointment in Levi's tone made Curt smile. He wasn't done with him yet by a long shot, but Levi didn't know that and Curt didn't want him to, just yet. "Easy, cowboy. I'll take care of you." Curt moved to the drawer where he'd stored his gear, taking out a length of hemp rope.

"What do you plan to do with that?"

"Tie you up." Levi's straining cock looked painfully aroused. He would take care of Levi soon enough. "On your back with your arms over your head." He glanced at the iron headboard above the bed. *Perfect.*

When Levi was in position, he tied his wrists together before looping them through the headboard.

"I've never been tied like a calf before."

"How do you like it?"

"Interesting. What are you going to do?"

"Play with you for a bit. I wish I had something to tie your ankles with too, but this will have to do."

"I'm already about to detonate, Curt."

"I know, but you won't come until I tell you to, will you, Levi."

"If you say so."

"I do and trust me, it will feel amazing when I'm through with you." He checked the tightness of the rope. "Not too tight?"

"No, although it's a bit scratchy."

Curt leaned in and licked Levi's neck, stopping when he centered on his mouth. "Go with the sensation. I plan to torture you for a bit. The scratchiness with heightened the pleasure of being tied so you have no control over what I do to you."

With Levi's secured, Curt licked from his lips to his cock, running his tongue over every inch of flesh exposed. He sucked on his nipples, enjoying how they tightened under his tongue. He nipped at the tender flesh until Levi moaned.

"You're killing me."

"But what a way to die, eh, my friend?" He kissed him full on the mouth, letting his tongue dance along the seam of Levi's lips. "Are you enjoying the torment?"

"Fuck yeah."

"Good."

Curt spent the next half an hour licking, sucking, and nibbling on Levi's skin before he finally took his engorged cock between his lips. The pulling of his mouth on the head of Levi's dick, made him push his hips up.

"Please. I need to come."

"In a minute." Curt took the length of Levi's cock into his mouth, going clear down until his nose brushed the hair at Levi's groin.

"Let me come, Curt. God, please."

Curt raked his teeth over the head of Levi's cock. "You may come in my mouth. Now, Levi, come now."

Levi's hips pushed up as a hearty moan escaped his mouth, then Curt's name.

The hot spurt of Levi's cum coated Curt's tongue as he lapped at Levi's cock. He slowly licked, and sucked until Levi's cock softened beneath his mouth.

"Oh my God," Levi whispered as his breathing slowed.

"I'm glad you liked it."

Levi exhaled sharply. "Liked it? I loved it. Something about being tied while you did that, was fucking amazing."

"Sometime, I'll have to let you tie me up and fuck me raw."

"Sounds good to me."

Curt decided to ask the question that had been bugging him since earlier. "I don't think you said. Are we sleeping together while we are at your place?"

"I planned to. I don't want to give this up just yet. We are pretty good together."

He nodded, liking the answer he received from the other man. "Good. I wanted to make sure we were on the same page because I'm sure I want this to go on for a bit yet." With a quick pull, Curt untied Levi. The slight rope burns on his wrists turned Curt inside out. He loved that look on someone under him. He kissed the burn marks, rubbing them to bring the circulation back into Levi's wrists. "These will fade by tomorrow, probably."

"I kind of like the look."

"I'm glad. I like them on you too."

"Are you into BDSM or something?" Levi asked, rubbing a particularly red spot on his left wrist.

"No, not in the true sense of the word although I do like tying people up and fucking them silly. Why?"

Levi shrugged his good shoulder. "Just asking. You seemed to know what you were doing with the rope and the fact that you had it handy, made me wonder a bit is all."

"I keep rope with me in case I need it for something with my gear. I haven't yet, but I figured it was better safe than sorry in any case."

"True."

"How is your shoulder? I was worried about putting you in that position with you having dislocated it a few days ago."

"It's fine. A little sore, but it didn't pop out again, which is good." He rotated the injured arm. "It feels pretty good, actually."

"I'm glad. You should be good to ride this weekend then." Curt grabbed his pants from the floor and slipped them on. "I guess Doc did a pretty good job on it with taping it."

"Yeah. Resting helped, I'm sure."

"I'm sure it did." Curt sat down in the chair near the small table. "Wow. I'm beat."

Levi smiled, showing off his sexy dimple in his right cheek. "Sex will do that to you."

"True." Curt smoothed the pant legs of his jeans with his palms. "Are you ready for bed?"

"I need to come down a bit, but I can watch television if you want to hit the sack."

"Sounds good." Curt was glad Levi had got a room with one bed. He kind of liked sleeping next to the other man. A warm body always made him sleep better. "I'm going to shower first." He grabbed some clean underwear and his pajama pants he usually slept in, before heading to the bathroom. "Care to join me?"

Levi grinned. "I think I need a break from all this sex. I haven't been this active in a long time."

"Damn." Curt slipped through the door, shutting it softly behind him.

As the water cascaded over his body, he let his mind drift. He liked the way the two of them got along, and the sex was amazing, but how would they do in close quarters living together? Was he really thinking long term with someone like Levi? How would that work on the circuit? They would have to keep their relationship very private. Otherwise, things would get mighty sticky and not in a good way, if the rest of the guys got wind they were in any kind of a semi-permanent situation. What about his family? They would probably freak. They had no idea of his sexual preferences and what if they found out he was into both men and women? Could he give up women altogether? He didn't think so. He like pussy on occasion, but to give it up, he didn't think he could. He really liked the way Levi's ass grabbed his cock when they fucked though. The slick slide of his cock through the grasping channel just did it for him. What about the walls of a nice, tight pussy?

He was completely confused at the moment as to which way he wanted his life to go. For now, he would have to play it by ear.

Chapter Seven

The next morning found them on the road to Levi's ranch. They would be there by ten, Levi couldn't wait. He hadn't been home in several weeks, hadn't seen his parents in that long either, and he wanted to check in on his baby sister who was about to pop out her first kid. He was going to be an uncle.

Wrought irons gates with a huge scrolling B came into view as they turned off the highway. He wondered how Curt liked the view of the property with its long, four board ranch fencing stretching for miles along the road. All of the property for a long section in both directions belonged to him. He'd bought the place over ten years before, when a family friend wanted to retire and move to the city. He managed to get the place for a great price, bringing the house back to its former glory, the barns back to great shape, and running his cattle and horses on the green pastures.

He loved his home and he was sure it showed in the pride he took in the surrounding area.

As they pulled up to the house, he realized the flowers along the porch railing were beginning to bloom. He would have to thank his housekeeper for tending to the beds for him. Of course, he knew she loved doing it so she would brush him off like she usually did.

The greying, large-bosomed woman came out wiping her hands on her apron as she squinted to see who was pulling up to the house. "Mr. Levi!" she shouted at the top of her lungs as she ran down the steps to meet him at the bumper of his truck. "I didn't know you were coming home or I would have had breakfast ready for you." She kissed him on the cheek. "I can whip up some biscuits and gravy for you though if you like. Men like you need a hearty breakfast." She took two steps backward. "I'll get started right now."

"No, Emma. It's fine. We ate in Oklahoma City before we came, but if you could, I would love some of your chicken and dumplings for lunch?"

She blushed bright red as she smiled so big, it almost took up her entire face. "You got it. I had chicken out for dinner anyways, so we'll have that for lunch and I'll run into town to get something else for dinner after we've finished lunch."

"You are a doll."

"Who is your friend?"

"This is Curt Walsh. He's a fellow rider on the circuit with me. We are going to be rooming together to save on money and since we were in Oklahoma City early, we thought we'd come out, do some chores, get on a couple of bulls, and relax for a few days."

Her gaze went from him to Curt and back. "Ah." She put her hands on her hips. "Welcome, Curt. I'm sure you'll have a wonderful time here on the home place. I'll get some coffee going. I'm sure you boys could use a cup."

"That would be great, Emma. I only had one cup with breakfast and you know I'm at least a pot a day drinker."

"Yes." She turned back toward the house before spinning back around. "The hands are already out in the pasture, but Nick is in the barn."

"Thanks. I'll go find him." He took several steps toward the barn, expecting Curt to follow. The other man fell into step beside him as he headed toward the big red structure in the distance. The barn was top of the line, with several horse stalls on each side of the main walkway, a hayloft, and large tack room. "Nick?"

"In the tack room."

They followed the sounds of whistling, making their way to the end of the long stretch where the door stood open. As they poked their heads through the doorway, Nick looked up from where he was cleaning tack.

"Hey, boss."

"How's things?"

"Good. Just doing some cleaning while the men are out moving the cattle to the upper pasture for a few days."

"This is Curt Walsh. He's a fellow rider. We've been traveling together to the event in Oklahoma City. Since we had a few days, we figured we would make the trek here to see what's going on, relax, do some chores, ride some practice bulls. You know."

"Sure, sure." Nick wiped at the soap clinging to the bridle in his hands. "How's the circuit?"

"Good. I won last weekend."

"I saw that. Watched it on television. You rode great."

"Thanks."

"Have you been to see your parents yet?"

"No. We just did the trip from the hotel to here. We'll probably go over there for dinner later or see them tomorrow." Levi's gaze traveled around the tack room. There were several bridles laid out for cleaning on the work bench to his left. Saddles lined the walls on the racks. Blankets hung off the saddles. Halters draped from nails in the walls. The whole place smelled like leather.

"I'm sure your momma will be happy to see you. You haven't been home for several weeks."

"I know." Country music played on the radio sitting on the shelf in the corner. "How's the wife and kids?"

"Doin' great. Everyone was sick with the flu last week, but they are better now."

"Well, that's good then. It must suck to have them all down at once."

"Yeah. We managed though."

Levi rocked back on his heels as he stuffed his hands in his pockets. "Well, we will leave you to your work. I've got some things to work on in the office." He glanced at Curt. "Do you want to do chores, watch television, or what?"

"Do you want me to take a look at your books? You mentioned that."

"Oh yeah. Okay. I'll give you something in the office to work on then."

"Great."

"See you after while, Nick. Let me know if you need anything, otherwise, I might not see you until the morning."

Nick nodded as he grabbed another bridle from the pile. "Sure, Levi. No problem. Enjoy your afternoon."

"Thanks."

He and Curt walked back down the aisle toward the front of the barn.

"This is a great setup you have here. Nice barn and stalls. This is fantastic." His head tipped back as he looked up to the rafters of the large building. "I haven't seen a barn this nice in a long time."

"I believe in taking care of the animals that take care of me."

"Your house is great too from what I saw."

"It's an old farmhouse built a long time ago. I did some upgrades to it when I bought it, but otherwise, it's pretty much the same as it was a hundred years ago. I've painted, dug out the garden so Emma could plant flowers, done some renovations on the inside, but not much. You'll like it, I think, especially if you like the old atmosphere."

They reached the edge of the barn to start across the lawn toward the house. He had to admit, he loved his house with the wraparound porch, pillars in the front, the swing to the left, and the old fashioned door on the front. The house had been painted white in the last year. Shutters were added this past summer in green since that was his favorite color. The porch rail and trim was painted the same color too.

He glanced back toward the rear of the house, where the kitchen window stood open, and white curtains blew in the breeze coming through from the front of the house. He knew Emma loved to open all the windows in the spring and fall, to catch the cross breeze.

Emma's humming could be heard through the window.

Levi smiled at the sound. He loved that old woman. She was something special.

Curt followed him toward the porch. They stopped and turned as a billowing cloud of dirt lifted into the air following a car barreling down the driveway at breakneck speed.

"What the fuck?"

"I don't know who could be hauling ass up my drive like that other than—my sister."

As the car stopped near the door and Rachel climbed out of the car, he smiled. She looked huge with her belly sticking straight out as she waddled up to the porch. "Levi!"

"What the hell, Rachel. You could have killed yourself driving like that."

"I had to come see you when Emma called Momma and told her you were home. I didn't know how long you'd be here and I didn't want to miss you." She grabbed him in a huge hug. "Lordy, I've missed you."

"I missed you too." He stepped back. "Look at you! You are getting bigger every day."

"If I don't pop this kid out shortly, I'm going to explode, I swear." She glanced at Curt, and then back to him. "Who is your friend?"

"Rachel, this is Curt. He's a fellow rider. We are traveling together to cut expenses and since we were close this weekend, he volunteered to come out to help me on the ranch."

Her perfectly arched eyebrow went up a notch. "Nice to meet you, Curt. Are you and Levi lovers?"

"Rachel!"

She laughed as she rubbed her protruding belly. "Well, why not. He's a cutie, Levi. You could do a lot worse, you know."

"Thank you, ma'am, but I think what's between me and Levi should stay between the two of us."

The smile gracing her face almost put the sun to shame. "You are!" She clapped enthusiastically. "How fabulous!"

"Knock it off, Rachel."

"What?"

"We don't need to broadcast anything all over the damned county, okay? Keep it on the down low, would you please?"

She zipped her lips with her fingers. "I won't say a word. I know how you are about your privacy."

"I have to be."

"I know. I'm sorry, but I think it's great you've found someone." She bounced on her toes like a small child wanting to ask questions as she put her hands behind her back. "Can I ask how long this has been going on?"

"Not long. A few days."

"Oh, how fun! New love."

"Easy, Rachel. We are lovers, nothing more."

"You never know how things will progress, brother. Keep an open mind."

Levi sighed and rolled his eyes. "Don't you have somewhere to be?"

"Nope."

Levi turned to Curt and said, "I think it's almost lunch time. Let's see what Emma has whipped up, and then we will get started on the books."

"Sounds good."

"It's chicken and dumplings."

"My favorite." Rachel replied, heading for the door.

"Where is your husband, by the way," he asked as they made their way in through the screen door, down the front hall and into the kitchen.

Rachel grabbed a biscuit off the side board, taking off a small bit to pop it into her mouth. "At work, of course. He's on patrol today."

He glanced at Curt who had taken a seat at the large dining room table. "Tim is an officer with the state patrol."

"Nice."

"Rachel is a school teacher at the local elementary school." He turned back toward Rachel. "Are you out on break or maternity leave since you are about to pop?"

She stuck another piece of biscuit into her mouth. "Maternity leave. This baby is due anytime and since my blood pressure has been up, they forced me to take off."

"Good idea."

"You look like you've dropped, Ms. Rachel. I bet that baby will be here in a day or two."

"You think so?"

"Yes, ma'am."

"You still don't know whether it's a boy or girl?" Levi asked, taking a seat at the table next to Curt as Emma began serving the meal.

"No."

"She's havin' a boy."

"You think so, Emma?"

"Yes. She's carrying that baby like a boy." Emma slid a bowl in front of Levi. "Little girls are carried like a basketball. She's got belly all the way around."

"I hope so. Tim wants a boy. I don't care either way."

"I bet you have him by the weekend."

"I wish. I'm so tired of being pregnant."

"How many children do you want, Rachel?" Curt asked before he spooned a mouthful of food between his lips.

"Three, but it will be some time before we have another one." She pushed her hair back off her forehead. "I've gained a lot of weight with this one which I want to lose before we go into baby number two." She took a bite of the chicken and dumplings, groaning as she swallowed. "Fabulous as always, Emma."

Emma brought a bowl for herself to the table after she served all of them, taking a seat at the opposite end from Levi.

Conversation went around the table about things on the ranch, how the hands were doing, how school had been for Rachel, and Levi's score during his last ride.

"Aren't you on the verge of qualifying for finals?" Emma spooned the last bit of her food into her mouth.

"Yeah. I need to keep winning to stay in the rankings."

"What about you, Curt?"

"I'm about three spots out right now so I need to win too."

Her eyebrow went up. "Sounds like some friendly competition going on between you two."

"Nah. If the points are there, we can both qualify easily enough," Curt answered.

Levi had finished his lunch and pushed the bowl away. "Curt is going to help me with the books. He says he's a numbers guy, so I'm hoping he can help me make sense of mine."

Rachel smiled as she finished her own meal. "He needs it."

"Thanks, sis."

"Well, you do." She looked at Curt. "He's terrible with keeping things straight. I try to help him as much as I can, but he's bad with keeping receipts for purchases, doing his payroll, and other stuff." She shrugged as she drank her milk. "I gave up on him a long time ago."

Curt smiled. "I'll get him straightened out."

"God, I hope so. He's a mess!"

"I love you too, Rachel."

She made smooching sounds toward him as she laughed. A few minutes later, she struggled to her feet as Levi jumped up to help her. "Thanks." She drained her glass and took the dishes to the sink. "I better get moving. My doctor's appointment is this afternoon. I'm hoping he says I'm ready right now. I could jump on that train easily enough." She waved as she headed for the door. "I'll see you later, Levi. Bye, Curt. Kisses to you, Emma. I'll let you know what he says and by the way, Momma expects you at supper tonight."

"I figured as much."

"Good. Bring Curt. She and Daddy will love to meet him." The door banged shut behind her as she headed for her car.

"Wow. She's like a tornado," Curt said as he leaned back in his chair.

"Yes she is, but I love her. She's always been there for me."

"She seems very supportive of your lifestyle."

"She is. She's totally cool with it."

Emma got to her feet, grabbed their bowls, and then moved toward the sink to do up the dishes. "I have supper on for the hands, but I won't expect you two for the meal since you'll be going to your folk's house."

"Thanks, Emma," Levi said as he stood. "Shall we tackle the books?"

"Sure." Curt followed close on his heels, down the hall toward his office.

Levi loved this room. It was his favorite in the house with its dark paneled walls, leather furniture, and large bookcase lining the wall to his right as they went through the door.

"What a great room."

"Thanks. It's my favorite."

"I can see why."

As Curt took in the room, Levi watched him. He really liked the way Curt didn't say anything, just looked around absorbing the atmosphere of the space. When his gaze came back to Levi's, the appreciation for everything around him was clear in his eyes.

"I love it. It's totally you."

"I think so."

Curt tilted his head to the side as his gaze slid down Levi's frame. "I'm going to fuck you on that desk, before we leave."

"You are?"

"Yep." Curt grinned. "Maybe before the day is out."

His cock responded as he thought about it. He wanted Curt to ream him as he bent over the edge of the desk. *Good God, I'm horny.*

"But, we have work to do before that happens, so show me your books."

For the next couple of hours, Curt bent over his shoulder as he tried to explain how he kept his records for the ranch. Curt made little clicking noises with his tongue every few minutes while he made notes on the pad of paper Levi had given him.

"Where are you tax records for last year?"

"In the filing cabinet."

"How did you file?"

"Single with the small business forms."

"Do you have corporate status?"

"No, should I?"

"Yes. You have employees you pay. It will help you in the long run to keep your taxes down with deductions."

"You realize you can't leave, right?"

Curt's eyes widened. "Leave?"

"I mean like ever because I'll never be able to keep this shit up if you do."

"No worries. You have me as long as you want me."

"Does that go for in the bedroom too?"

"Yep."

"What about you wanting pussy every now and then?"

"I'll manage without it."

"For now?"

"For now." Curt pulled Levi's chair away from the desk. "Open your fly."

"Is the door locked?" Levi asked, unzipping his jeans and pushing them as well as his boxers down to mid-thigh. His aching cock sprang free. The moan escaping his mouth sounded primal even to him.

"No and I'm not going to. The possibility of getting caught is half the fun." Curt slid to the floor on his knees, took Levi's cock in his hand, and stroked the ridged shaft several times. "You are so hard."

"For you."

"Only me."

"Yes. I haven't been this horny in a long time."

Curt enveloped his cockhead between his lips, sucking strongly as Levi's hips bucked beneath his mouth. The suction he was performing had Levi on edge in seconds. His balls tingled. His cock ached. His head felt like it would explode at any time if Curt didn't finish him off. He'd been horny since they left the hotel this morning after seeing Curt in nothing but a towel when he came out of the bathroom. Levi wanted to jump him then, but he knew they needed to get on the road, so he resisted much to the disappointment of his throbbing cock.

As Curt worked Levi's dick, Levi lost himself in the sensations of Curt's mouth. The suck and pull drew his desire to a baser need. He wanted to come down Curt's throat in a hot spurt of come before letting Curt push him over the desk and fuck him hard.

"Now, please. Make me come, now."

"Are you there?" Curt asked, glancing up through his eyelashes as he licked Levi's dick with his tongue.

"Oh, fuck yeah."

"Then come for me. Paint my tongue."

Levi exploded on a rush of semen that spurted across Curt's tongue and down his throat. The other man groaned his pleasure as he continued to lick and suck until every drop disappeared. After he gave him one last swipe of his tongue, Curt stood, shoved his jeans and shorts to the floor before he said, "Over the desk."

Levi surged to his feet, bent at the waist over the edge of his desk, and spread his ass cheeks. "Lube?"

"You're lucky. I have a small tube in my pants pocket. I wouldn't want to do a dry slide."

"Please don't."

"If you aren't into masochism, then I wouldn't. I'm not a sadist wanting to hurt you."

"Good."

A dollop of lube hit his crack, sliding down until it almost dripped off his balls before Curt smeared it up and into his ass. Levi moaned as Curt's finger penetrated through the ring of muscles.

"Ready?"

"Fuck yeah."

Curt pushed the head of his dick into Levi's ass, slowly piercing the hole with his entire shaft before Levi sighed in completion. When Curt was all the way in, Levi had the intense urge to push back against the invading cock. "Easy, cowboy."

"Move. Please. I need this."

"So do I." Curt began the slow glide in and out of his ass.

Levi thought he would lose his mind. Even though he'd already had one orgasm, his cock filled again at the sensations happening in his ass. Good God, he loved this feeling. The sweet burn of penetration just did it for him on a primal level he couldn't get enough of. As the thrusts of Curt's hips sped up, Levi groaned in satisfaction. It felt amazing and he never wanted it to end.

Chapter Eight

Spending time at Levi's parents place was a weird affair for Curt. He knew he liked Levi's parents when his mother hugged him and kissed him on the cheek like she was welcoming him into the family.

He wasn't ready for that.

They seemed like nice people though. They fully accepted Levi's lifestyle from what he could tell. Unlike how he thought his parents would react should they find out about the men or man in his life. He only had one man these days and he kind of liked it that way. Levi seemed like a good match for him in the sex department and they got along so far in personalities, with him being the more dominant one in the relationship, but he didn't know how they would get on when it came to something deeper. Did he want deeper? H didn't think so, at least not right now. He did like the fact of being part of Levi's ranch. It almost felt like home.

"You okay?" Levi asked, sitting beside him on the sofa as they waited for supper to be ready.

Curt could hear Levi's mom softly humming in the kitchen. He loved the sound. "Yeah, I'm fine. I'm amazed at your family. They are so supportive."

"Yes, they are. I love them a lot."

"Do you have other siblings besides Rachel?"

"No. It was just her and me growing up." Levi laughed. "It was kind of funny because when I came out as gay, I got a lot of flack at school. Rachel was constantly beating people up defending me. The town seems to be okay with it now, as long as I'm not in their faces I guess. A few more people have come out as gay since I did, but it's still not widely accepted. They kind of ignore us."

"How would that work should you bring a partner home to live with you?"

Levi shrugged. "I don't know. Most of my friends are fine with it. There were a few people who openly sneered. For the most part, it would be okay, I guess." He leaned against the couch, putting his arm along the back. "It's a small town. You know how folks are in small towns."

"I know, that's why I asked." Curt picked at the seam of his pressed jeans. "I'm not sure how folks would be in my hometown."

"Here, the mayor came out gay in the last few years so it's kind of an accepted thing more so now than it would have been fifteen years ago when I came out."

"That's great to hear. When someone of importance comes out, it tends to be a little more tolerated by the people in town."

"Yep."

"Supper is ready, boys," Levi's mother called from the kitchen.

"Be right there, Mom."

"Levi, can you call your father from the barn, please?"

"Sure," he said, climbing to his feet. "Be right back, Curt."

"No problem. I'll help your mom set the table."

"I'm sure she would love that."

Curt headed into the kitchen as Levi walked to the front door. "Can I help?"

"Sure, son. There are plates in the cupboard there to your right. If you wouldn't mind grabbing four and setting the table, I would be very appreciative."

"Sure, ma'am." Curt reached up, grabbed the plates, and walked to the large farm table with six chairs around it. They obviously liked to entertain with such a big table and only four in the family. "Any particular place you want these?"

"No, just one on the end for Dad. The rest can go wherever. You and Levi can sit together if you like." She stirred the potatoes she had going in the cast iron skillet. "How long have you two been a couple?"

"We aren't really a couple."

"You aren't?"

"Well, no. I mean yes, I guess we are, sort of, but it's only been a few days since we started, uh, seeing each other."

She smiled before turning back around to finish dinner. "You two are cute together. I hope things work out between you."

"I don't know if anything will come of this or not. We are taking things one day at a time."

"Good. That's best, I think." She glanced over her shoulder. "Would you put the silverware on the table too? It's in the drawer to your left by the refrigerator."

He frowned. She seemed okay with his explanation of his and Levi's relationship, for what it was worth. "Sure."

After he set the utensils on the table, he found the cupboard with the glasses in it as she finished up supper and put it on the table, just as he heard Levi and his father come through the door.

"There now."

Supper was lively as he sat and watched the way Levi's parents laughed, teased, and ribbed him.

Curt wondered what it would be like to have that kind of relationship with his family. They weren't like that at all. They were pretty straight-laced conservatives who didn't kid around with the family at all. His dad ranched the home place while his mom worked as a legal secretary in town for a local attorney. His parents were okay, he guessed, but they sure didn't seem to support him in anything he tried including bull riding. They worked all the time, never really caring what he did after school and on weekends. They cared more about his sister, than him by far. Now, his sister was on drugs from what he could gather, living on welfare, didn't know who the fathers of her four kids were, and constantly asked him for money. He loved his family, but they didn't seem like they loved him in return.

He smiled as the interaction continued.

"How is the riding going, Levi," his dad asked. "I saw the win last weekend. That was great."

"Yeah. I'm last in line to go to the finals right now, so I need every point to stay there." He glanced next to him. "Curt's hanging in there too. A win for him would be helpful."

"I hope you both win." His mother laughed. "I guess that's not possible, but you can both be up there on the top, right?"

Levi smiled at his mother. "Yes, Mom."

She turned at looked at him. "Where are you from, Curt?"

"Amarillo, ma'am."

"That's not far at all!"

"No, ma'am."

The food was fabulous. The steak was perfect, melting on his tongue as he took another bite. The meat had just the right amount of seasoning, cooked to perfection, and so tender, you could almost cut it with a fork.

"No need to say ma'am around me. I'm Donna to everyone, including you." She pointed to Levi's father.

"And he's Charles or Mom and Dad if you are so inclined." She smiled before putting another bite of food in her mouth. "We've adopted many of the kids' friends over the years."

Charles pushed his plate way. "What are your plans while you're home, Levi?"

"Doin' some chores, working on some practice bulls, you know, ranch stuff. Curt is going to go over my books. He's a financial wizard, so he's going to get me straightened out." Levi finished his food, but sat sipping his soda.

Curt liked how Levi trusted him to get his finances in order. Trust wasn't an easy thing and after he'd already been taken before, it would be harder. He knew he would have a hard time trusting someone in Levi's shoes. "I'm not a wizard, but I do have some knowledge of ranch finances. My parents have a place. I snuck into my dad's books while he wasn't looking. He wasn't really supportive of me doing much of anything, but numbers I could do. After a while, he reluctantly let me do the books sometimes. I don't know what he plans to do with the ranch when he retires." He took a drink of his milk. "He probably won't retire for several years yet anyway."

"Is your mom a housewife or does she work outside of the home?" Donna asked.

"She's a legal secretary to an attorney in Amarillo. She never did stay home with us kids except when we were babies. She went back to work as soon as she could after we were a few months old."

"Do you have siblings?"

"A sister. Like your family, there were just the two of us. She's living in Amarillo with her kids. She's not married or anything though."

"I see." Donna's face lit up. "Our Rachel is about to have our first grandbaby."

"Rachel came by the house today, Mom."

"Doesn't she look radiant?"

"Yeah, but she's miserable. I hope she has the baby soon. Emma thinks she will any day now."

"Emma is a pretty good judge of that sort of thing." Donna stood, grabbed everyone's plate, and moved to the kitchen sink. "She's delivered a few babies in her lifetime."

"Has she?"

Donna rinsed the few dishes after she'd cleaned off the food, and slid them into the dishwasher. "Yes. She used to be a mid-wife several years ago, before she retired when the hospital came in. There wasn't much of a need for one after the women started going there to deliver their babies."

"I never knew that about her."

"She loves taking care of you these days. When you have children of your own, she'll be like a grandmother to them."

"It's kind of hard for a gay man to have children, Mom."

"Not so. I hear about a lot of gay couples adopting children or doing surrogacy with someone to carry for them." She turned around as she wiped her hands on the dishtowel. "I've been doing some research on the subject."

Levi's eyebrow rose. "Why are you doing research on it?"

She put the dishtowel on the counter all folded neatly. "Because I'm sure someday, you'd like to have a couple of kids. Am I right?"

"I guess." He glanced at Curt. "I really hadn't thought about it. I'd like to have a partner first and now that gay marriage is legal in Oklahoma, I hope to be able to marry."

"Well after marriage comes children."

Levi shook his head and laughed. "Yes, Mom, in a normal relationship, but it's a lot more difficult in a gay relationship."

"What do you think, Curt?"

"Uh—" He kind of sputtered. "I hadn't really thought about it either."

"Do you want children someday?"

"Sure, but since I'm not planning to retire from the circuit for several more years, it hasn't been a priority for me. Like Levi, it's hard to wrap my brain around marriage and kids right now." He really didn't want to get into the fact that he wasn't completely gay either. His preferences really didn't matter in this scenario. Plus, if he really thought about it, he wasn't sure he would marry a man or a woman. In this case, he was with Levi and they were enjoying the sexual relationship they had currently, but what if he found a woman he really loved? Could he walk away from being with men?

The conversation switched to ranching and Curt sighed. He really didn't want to think beyond this week. He wanted to enjoy the time with Levi, his family, and the ranch, ride a couple of bulls to get warmed up for this weekend, and maybe have some fun between the sheets. Serious thoughts weren't on his agenda.

When they returned to the ranch that evening, the sun had already set, ranch work was done, and the hands had gone on home except for the foreman. Nick met them on the porch where he sat smoking a cigarette and enjoying a beer. "Did you two enjoy supper with your momma?"

"Sure did. How did things go here today?"

"Just fine. Cattle are down in the outer pasture. The boys got them all settled in, fixed a couple of spots that were weak in the fence, cleaned the barn stalls out, and bedded down the horses for the night. I got all the tack cleaned today too." Nick snuffed out the butt of his cigarette in the ashtray sitting near his elbow. "I'll be heading home now."

"Thanks for staying until we got back. I didn't realize we would be gone so long."

Nick laughed as he climbed to his feet. "I figured as much. Your folks like to talk, especially when you're home." He walked down the two stairs of the porch, but stopped at the bottom to turn back around. "I'll be here at six. We've got a load of supplies coming in. I'll need to be here to inventory them."

"Great."

"Enjoy your evenin'." Nick walked to his truck, opened the door, and then slid inside, shutting it behind him. The engine turned over a moment later, before he backed up, and headed down the driveway.

"You got lucky with your foreman."

"Yeah, I know. He's a nice guy, hard worker, and knows ranching like the back of his hand."

Curt walked toward Levi, pushing him back against the side of the house with his body. "Is Emma still here?"

"No." Levi's breath came out in a rush.

"Good." Curt slammed his mouth down on Levi's, crushing his lips beneath his as he ground his lips against Levi's. He wanted it rough, needed it hard, and he planned to fuck Levi down and dirty tonight. He hoped his lover didn't mind.

Levi panted hard from the kiss and when Curt cupped his cock in his hand, Levi groaned, pushing the hard flesh against his hand. The hornier the better, Curt figured, and he knew he was on the verge of losing it in his pants at the moment.

When he lifted his mouth, he growled, "Bedroom. Now."

Levi scooted past him, opened the screen, and walked into the main hall. The place was dark except for one lamp left on in the living room. As Curt followed him, they made their way up the stairs at the end of the long hall, to the second floor. The bedroom stood off to the right. He didn't have to wait long after they entered the room for Levi to work his jeans off his hips, freeing the length of his cock to Curt's view. He loved the long, thick shaft of Levi's cock.

The moment Levi had his pants off, along with his socks and boots, Curt fell to his knees to take the length of flesh between his lips. Sucking Levi was one of the joys of this relationship and he intended to enjoy it tremendously. He licked at the pre-cum leaking from the tip before taking the entire shaft in his mouth. The purple head of Levi's cock looked painfully swollen with need, but he planned to enjoy sucking him until he was ready to explode.

The moans coming from Levi's lips encouraged Curt to continue his ministrations to Levi's cock. When Levi wrapped his fingers in Curt's hair, he groaned at the pull on his scalp. Every once in a while, he liked being the one on the bottom, but this time, he planned to appreciate the man beneath him with everything in him.

Levi's breathing sped up, telling Curt he was close to coming, but Curt didn't want him to come until he was deep in his ass. He pulled back, licking slowly along the front of Levi's dick, waiting for Levi's to come down off the ledge.

"You are a bastard, you know that?"

"Nope. My momma was married to my daddy when I was born." Curt laughed as he sat back on his haunches. "On the edge of the bed, feet up, knees to your chest. I want to see that puckered hole just waiting for me to ram my dick inside."

"Do it."

"I plan to in a second. I need some lube and a condom."

"Lube yes, but you can go bare if you want. I'm clean. I trust you."

Surprise ricocheted through him. He didn't think Levi would let him go bare, but man, he wanted to so he could feel that silky slide of his cock into Levi's ass. "Are you sure? I'm clean. I was tested about six months ago. I do it every time I change partners."

"Yes, I'm sure. I can't wait to feel that little ball."

"Okay then." Curt grabbed the lube and trickled some down the crack of Levi's ass.

The hole spasmed from the cooler liquid against his skin. The sight turned him into jelly, it was so fucking sexy.

Curt quickly shed his clothes in his haste to be inside Levi. His cock hurt. He needed this so badly, his balls ached. Had it only been this afternoon since he'd been inside this man? The connection was so strong he didn't know how he would walk away when the time came. For now, he would enjoy the attentions of his friend and lover, to the fullest.

Positioned at Levi's hole, he slicked up his dick before slowly pushing inside. The sensation amazed him. The slide of his piercing against the slick walls of Levi's channel made him shudder in response. He'd never felt anything like it. The groan escaping from his own lips made him realize Levi moaned in return.

"Fuck yeah."

He pushed until his cock was completely engulfed in Levi. "Oh, my God."

"You can say that again, but right now, I need you to move. Please, God, move, Curt. You're killing me, here."

Curt slowly withdrew his cock only to push it back in a second later. The slow glide tortured him with the intensity of the feeling. Goose bumps broke out on his skin. Cold sweat trickled down his back as he leaned into Levi. The passion between them amazed him. He couldn't believe he'd connected with his friend in such a manner that all he wanted to do was fuck him silly, sleep curled up with him in bed, and wake up side-by-side in the morning.

With each thrust of his hips, he brought his desire to an explosive ending. He didn't know how much longer he could hold on without coming hard inside Levi's ass. "Are you ready?"

"Hell yeah. I'm about to lose it."

"Come with me, then. I want to see you paint your cum all over your abdomen and chest."

"Fuck!" Levi exploded. White spurts of cum streamed across his skin as Curt detonated himself inside Levi with a deep groan of satisfaction.

As they both came down off their temporary high, Curt wondered where they went from here? Would their lives intertwine? Would they stay in this relationship a while before moving on to find new lovers? Right now, he didn't want anyone else and if it was up to him, they would stay this way for a good long while. Did that mean he was falling in love with Levi? Nah. That couldn't be it.

* * * *

"So, Curt. Where do we go from here?" Levi asked, lowering his legs as Curt slowly withdrew his cock from his ass.

"I'm not sure I know what you mean."

"Are we going to stay lovers on the circuit?"

"Sure, why not?"

"What about keeping it from the other riders? It might get difficult."

"But if we're rooming together anyway, they won't think twice about it. We just won't be able to touch, kiss, or anything like that while we are around the other guys," Curt said from the bathroom off the back of the bedroom where he'd went to clean up.

Levi sat up on the bed. "You do realize Jefferson wants you, right?"

"He does?"

Levi frowned as he stood to find a towel to wipe himself off with after their rousing bout of sex. "Hell yeah, he does. He got all pissy with me at the last stop after you left breakfast wanting to know if I was doing you."

"What did you say?" Curt asked, wiping the lube from his dick before throwing the towel to Levi.

"No, of course. We weren't lovers then." Levi caught the piece of cotton in his fist. The slimy goop came off easily with the rough towel.

"Was he really demanding about it?"

Levi didn't like the way this conversation seemed headed. He didn't want Curt even thinking about Jefferson as a potential partner while they were fucking, but it's not like they had talked about exclusivity. Maybe they should. "Yes, he was." Levi pulled his pants back on. "You know, if you really are interested in Jefferson, let me know. I'll back off."

Curt had pulled on his underwear before rounding on Levi. "I don't want Jefferson. I want you." He crushed his mouth against Levi's in a lip splitting kiss. The demand behind the gesture was apparent. Curt wanted him. "Curiosity got the best of me. I'm not interested in anyone else, but it's flattering to think someone wants you, Levi."

"I'm not jealous."

"Yes you were."

Levi looked deep into Curt's dark brown eyes. He wasn't sure what he saw except the temporary need building inside both of them. He knew he wanted Curt and he liked having the other man around, but where did they go from here? For now, it seemed they had a partnership of sorts, lovers definitely, and were in a relationship. What happened when the whole thing fell apart, he didn't want to fathom. He'd cross that path when the time came. "Okay. I guess I am a little jealous. We are kind of in a relationship, right?"

"Yeah, I guess." Curt pulled on his pants as he looked around for his socks.

"You guess?"

He turned to face Levi. "Listen, Levi, don't put a lot of stock into what we have. It's new. It's scary. It's different from what I've had before, but I can't even think about anything beyond the here and now. I have too much going on in my life to think about the future beyond next week or the week after with finals coming. That's where my focus is. What we've got is good, don't get me wrong. I like you and I think the sex between us is fantastic, but I'm not into putting labels on things. Not now."

Levi's heart did a little flip. He wasn't sure what Curt meant, but he had a guess. Levi wasn't ready to put labels on things between them yet either. It was too soon. For now he would go with the flow, have some great sex with Curt, and see where things went.

Chapter Nine

While they rode back toward Oklahoma City, Levi reflected on the last couple of days. They worked side-by-side doing chores, riding fences, working on the books, and loving the nights away. Levi thought things were going great. He'd really learned a lot from Curt on the finances of the ranch, realizing he was in better shape financially than he thought. Of course, he wanted Curt to keep doing the books, but that would mean a permanent type relationship between them and neither of them wanted to look that far into the future.

With it only being a little over an hour by car, they didn't need to go until later in the morning. The rides started at eight in the evening, but they wanted to have a few hours to schmooze with the fans hanging around, work out, and warm up.

The venue was a large arena in Oklahoma City where they'd done a run before. This was a venue they did every year, and so far, every year, his rides had sucked. He hoped this was his year. So far, he'd ridden his last six bulls without being bucked off. He needed a good weekend, and so did Curt.

"You ready for this?"

"Yep. Ready as I'll ever be," Curt replied as they worked the rosin into their bull ropes at the back of the chutes right before the rides began.

They still needed to do their introductions to the crowd, which they did in the middle of the arena, but he was ready, loose, and confident. "Me too."

"I'll be your spotter in the chutes if you want me to."

"Sure. I'll do the same for you, of course."

"Good." Curt nodded, his hat shading his eyes while he bent to his task.

This venue was absolutely amazing. The crowds loved bull riders here and they loved the crowds. Soon the introductions would be made and the group would soak up every cheer. It was part of being in the limelight, he figured. One he loved like everyone else on the circuit.

Jefferson walked by, giving Levi a sideways glance before taking a long look at Curt where he was bent over at the waist working his chaps over his legs. Curt has a great ass, rounded in all the right places, with great assets in his Wranglers. *God, I love Wranglers.*

"What the hell are you staring at, Jefferson?" Curt snarled as he turned around. "Beat it."

Jefferson scooted along like a dog with his tail between his legs and a frown on his face. He obviously didn't like being put in his place by Curt. Levi did. He loved the way Curt told the other man off.

"You're lookin' might smug, Levi," Curt said as he finished fastening his chaps.

"Nope. Not me." Levi grinned, feeling the smug look he knew rested on his lips. *Okay, I admit to it. I really like Curt.*

The guys gathered by ranking on the circuit, with the last guy out being whoever held first place in the world standings Levi was third to the last coming out since he was the winner from the week before. The three guys behind him were the top three in the standings. He hoped he'd be there in a couple of weeks. None of the rankings were very far apart in point totals. It was anyone's game.

After all the guys were introduced, everyone got into place. Levi would be riding almost last in the first round.

He'd drawn a pretty good bull, one who spun a lot into his riding hand, which made it much easier for him to stay on the bull, but one who gave the fans a good show. Those things meant he might get a good score if he stayed on for his full eight.

Curt drew a harder bull to ride. He would have a great score, should he ride the entire time.

Before their respective rides, he tried to avoid spending any alone time with Curt. He didn't want the other riders to get wind of the change in their relationship since he didn't know how they would react to it. There would be a few haters, he knew, but he hoped the majority would accept it for what it was. Hell, he didn't even know what it was, but he would try to ride it out for however long Curt wanted it to be.

When Curt's turn came up to ride, he settled himself on the back of the bull with his bull rope. The fence man helped him tighten the rope around the bull while Levi spotted him with his vest in case the bull jumped or something. It was a precautionary measure for the safety of the rider.

Curt wore a helmet to ride, although several of the riders didn't. Levi thought they were foolish not to. He'd seen a rider killed when his head snapped back and hit the back end of the bull, breaking his neck in the process. The kid was only twenty when it happened, way too young to die. It had put the fear of God in Levi as they carried the kid off the dirt on a stretcher.

This was a rough sport anyway, but to watch that, just wow. God forbid it happen again even though injuries were part of the sport. Levi knew all too well as he rotated his shoulder, hoping it would stay put in the socket for a few more weeks. After finals, he would get it worked on.

After Curt wrapped his rope around his hand, he pounded on his fingers to help tighten his grip on the rope. He nodded quickly, telling the guy holding the catch on the fence to release the bull.

With his left hand whipping back and forth, Curt held on. The bull spun to the right, before doubling back to spin to the left, still his rider wouldn't budge.

The buzzer sounded, indicating Curt had managed his full eight.

Levi cheered as the crowd went wild with applause. Curt pumped his fists in the air before he ran for the fence to get out of the way of the bull, which made his way into the exit chute. Curt went around to the exit for the riders and made his way back to the dressing rooms. His day was done. Levi still had to ride, but he knew his friend would be back in a few minutes to help him with his own ride.

Meanwhile, Levi watched the rest of the riders. Some made the buzzer, others didn't.

Break time.

There was always a break in the action about midway through the listings for the day. Since Levi's ride was one of the last, he headed for the john. He needed to take a piss bad since he'd drank two full sodas on the way back from the ranch.

"You ready?" Curt asked, meeting him as he hit the corner of the dressing room

"In a minute. I've got to take a piss before I ride. I'm up third after the break."

"All right."

Levi went around the corner, past the other riders, and into the backroom where the urinals were located. A couple of other guys were standing around, one washing his hands, while another stood at the urinal to the left. Levi took the one to the right.

"How is your shoulder, Levi?"

"Feeling pretty good tonight, Tate. How are you doing?"

"Good. Ready to ride."

"Me too." As soon as he finished, he washed his hands before heading back out to behind the chutes to strap on his chaps. He wanted to watch the other guys ride while he got ready, so he'd grabbed them from his gear bag after he'd went to the bathroom.

He stopped near the back of the chutes where his bull rope hung from the gate, and worked his chaps around his legs to strap them on. Next came the buckle around his hips. Chaps kept their legs protected like the vest kept their chest protected. They needed all this gear in case the bull decided to try to gore them. It happened before and lucky for the cowboy, he'd had on protective gear.

"Next up, Levi Bond."

Curt nodded from his position as the spot man when Levi climbed the fence to position himself on the bull. Once he'd lowered his body onto the back of the two-thousand pound animal, the contractor secured the bull rope around the bull's chest, before handing the slack off to the guy next to him to tighten it. Levi wound the end around his hand, pulling it tight across his palm. He pounded on his fingers to help his grip, yanked his chaps up out of his way, and nodded for the gate keeper to release the bull.

Time stopped.

The bull jumped straight up, landing on all fours with a teeth-jarring, ear-ringing bounce before doing it again. *Holy shit!*

He whipped to the right, into Levi's riding hand, spinning in circles a few times as he kicked straight out behind him.

The buzzer sounded. He'd done it!

He released his hand from the rope before jumping clear of the kicking bull. He glanced up to see what his score was. Eighty-nine point two four. He'd even received a good score although it didn't put him in first place. He was in third with Curt in fourth. They would be bucking in the final round, which meant as long as they went for eight in the final go round, they both might gain on the leaders. Those numbers meant everything at this stage of the game. If the guys who were hanging onto those last remaining spots in the final thirty-five didn't finish both rides this weekend, they would gain ground.

Several of the other riders didn't get a qualifying ride in round one, but would have a chance to ride again in round two. The top fifteen scores would advance to the championship round. Both he and Curt would have to qualify in round two if they wanted that world championship run.

Curt met him at the back of the chutes. "You did great."

"Thanks."

"I believe you're third right now, but the scores are so close, it doesn't make much difference."

"Yeah, that bull was crazy. Did you see that jump? I nearly cracked a tooth with the bone-jarring plant he did."

"I saw it. I wondered if he rattled your bones with that one."

"He sure did."

"Ready for round two?"

"Yeah. I hope the bull I got this time is good. I haven't heard of him before."

"How is your shoulder holding up?"

He held the shoulder and rotated it around twice. "Fine. It felt good on the ride."

"That's great." Curt slapped him on the left shoulder. "Are we going to check out the bar after the event tonight? It'll be kind of late when we get done since this one didn't start until eight."

"I'm game if you are. I could use a beer after that ride."

"I can imagine so."

They climbed up on the back of the chutes to watch the last rider. Rusty Arnold was the reigning world champion and he also held the top spot in the standings this year. All of the top riders were within a few hundred points of each other, so it was still anyone's game this year.

Rusty drew a bull that only five riders had ever ridden in this round. He'd managed to best the beast a few years before with a score of ninety-two point five. This match up was important. If he rode this bull for the full eight, he would be in the second round with a great shot of hitting the final round. If he won for the weekend, he'd be almost unstoppable in the world championships.

Levi held his breath as Rusty gave the nod. The bull came straight out, charging one of the bull fighters first, kicking his feet out behind him as he bucked hard. Rusty held on, his right hand waving like a flag as he moved with the bull each time it changed direction. It was no wonder Rusty was the world champion. He made it look like child's play.

When the buzzer sounded, the crowd went wild. Rusty pulled his rope, but his hand was hung up in the grip. He'd tied a suicide wrap, the stupid bastard.

As the bull continued to buck, Rusty was flung side to side like a ragdoll. His hat went flying. His legs swung back and forth as if there were no bones in them.

Everyone heard a snap as the bull stepped on his lower leg when the bull fighters had finally managed to get him loose, but not out of danger.

Shit. He may be out for the season.

No one wished injury on the other riders, not even to further their own career.

"Did you hear that?" Curt asked.

"Yeah. I think the bull stepped on him and snapped his leg in two."

"Holy shit. That could cost him the season."

"Yeah, I know."

While the medical team came out to tend to Rusty, his score flashed on the board. Ninety point zero. It was a hell of a score, but at what cost? They wouldn't know until the doctor had a chance to look at him.

To his credit, Rusty waved from the stretcher, indicating he was conscious and doing okay for the moment. Bull riders were a tough breed. He would more than likely be out at least for a few weeks.

After the ground was clear, they resumed riding, getting the second go round under way. The final round would happen tomorrow with the top fifteen riders going into the championship for the weekend.

Levi was on a roll. He just hoped he could maintain his momentum and keep his streak alive.

The beginning of round two saw him draw one of the toughest bulls on the circuit, the one who had dislocated his shoulder the week before. Mr. Tough. He hoped he could do it again for another good score without injuring himself. He couldn't afford to get hurt again, otherwise he would be in the same boat as Rusty, possibly out for the season.

When it came his turn to ride, he slid into position on the back of the bull, wrapped his hand, and gave the nod.

The world exploded in two thousand pounds of mean bull.

Levi did everything he could to stay on for the required eight seconds. It wasn't a pretty ride, but it would do.

The buzzer sounded.

He released his hand and jumped clear. When he saw his score, he pumped his fists in the air to celebrate. He was in first place.

Curt had already ridden and managed to ride to the buzzer, giving him a combined score just below Levi's. They were number one and number two for the weekend, two of several competitors to ride their bulls in the second round to advance to the final. If he won this weekend, he might even manage to catapult himself into a good standing in the world championship race.

After grabbing his bull rope from the bull fighters, he headed for the exit. He walked around the back of the chutes to be met by several of the other riders. One in particular, he'd always found attractive, but he didn't know which way the guy swung so he never approached him.

Butch slapped him on the left shoulder. "Hey, Levi. That was a fantastic ride."

"Thanks, Butch. Sorry you didn't qualify this weekend."

"No matter. It happens. I'm still in the races so I'm happy." Butch tipped his hat back on his head. "Did you go home this weekend? I know you're from somewhere not too far."

"Yeah. I spent a couple of days on my place before coming back in this afternoon. It's only a little over an hour home from here."

"Wow. That's great." Butch looked down at the tips of his boots. "Did Curt go with you? I know you two caravanned into this event."

"Yeah. He helped me out at my place."

He glanced back up to catch Levi's gaze. "Cool. I hear you two are rooming together."

"That's the plan. We both need to cut back on expenses."

"I know the feeling. I was looking for someone to room with too."

Levi itched his leg, before reaching down to unhook the buckle on his chaps. "Sorry if you were thinking of asking Curt."

"Actually, I was thinking of asking you."

"Oh?"

"Yeah." Butch leaned closer. "I'd like to talk to you about something."

"What's that?"

Butch's gaze shifted around to several of the other riders within earshot. "Not here. Too many ears."

Curiosity got the best of him. "Okay."

"Meet me at the bar later? We can chat in the corner where our conversation will be drowned out by all the other noise around."

"Sure."

"Great. See you there." Butch disappeared down the hallway toward the locker rooms.

Levi shrugged. *Weird.* His gaze caught Curt's from where he stood against the chutes. Curt's eyes narrowed slightly. *I wonder what that look is for.*

Several other riders came over to congratulate him on his ride as he unhooked his chaps the rest of the way, making him feel great. He liked being on the top, figuratively.

During sex, he liked being on the bottom, although the top was good sometimes too. Lucky for him, Curt seemed to prefer the dominate position in their relationship. Curt sidled over with that slow, hip swinging walk of his. Levi's mouth watered as he watched the approach. Curt's cock was outlined by his jeans where it laid against his pelvis. Levi had never noticed before they'd become lovers, but Curt had an impressive cock.

"What did Butch want?"

"I don't know. He said he wanted to talk to me about something, but mostly he was congratulating me on the ride."

"You did well. Great score."

"Thanks." Levi wrapped his chaps up in a roll. He needed to get his gear bag from the locker room. "You ready to go back to the hotel?"

"Yeah."

They headed for the back room together. "Your ride was text book."

"I did make it look easy this round."

"Yes, you did."

"Too bad about Rusty."

"What did you hear?"

"He'll be out for at least a couple of weeks. They don't think he'll be back for the season, more than likely. The break was a bad one."

"Wow. He'll lose his chance to get back to back championships this year."

Levi headed for the corner of the locker room where his bag lay open. He stuffed his chaps inside, zipped it up, and flung it over his good shoulder. Curt grabbed his from nearby before they headed out toward the parking lot.

Several fans lined the ropes.

"Levi!"

He turned to see a twenty-something brunette holding a marker. "Can you sign my bag for me?"

"Sure."

She was kind of pretty with her hair hanging down in long, flowing curls around her face, big green eyes, a pretty mouth lined with red lipstick, and a top that emphasized her breasts. Too bad she wasn't his type. Curt might like her though.

"Curt, will you sign it too, please?"

"Of course, darlin'."

The girl nearly melted on the pavement as she giggled.

Some of the other riders came out behind them. The fans cheered as each rider spent time with them for pictures and autographs. This was part of being a rider. He loved it. The part of being with the fans made it all worthwhile in his book.

As they made their way toward the end of the crowd, Levi caught Curt's gaze as he tipped his head to the side indicating they should make a break for the truck. The hotel wasn't far, but he wanted to go back to the room to take a shower before they went to the bar for a couple of beers.

His throat felt parched from the dust and dirt of the arena, one of the hazards of being a bull rider. He knew he had a brown coating of grime on his clothes. Clean jeans, a nice button down shirt and dusty boots made the women go crazy. He laughed. Totally not what he was after.

He glanced at Curt as they walked to the truck. *I wonder if there is time for a quick fuck?*

When they'd both slid into the cab of his truck, he turned the engine over before pulling out of the parking lot.

"I need a shower before we go to the bar."

"Yeah, me too. This dirt is making my skin itch."

Curt looked relaxed sitting in the seat beside him, but Levi got the impression he was strung tight for some reason. Maybe it was the way his fist lay clenched on his thigh. Maybe it was the slow tick in his jaw or the narrowing of his eyes as he glanced around.

Silence hung thick in the air between them on the short ride to the hotel. Levi didn't know what he'd done wrong, but apparently Curt was pissed about something.

Chapter Ten

They made their way into the hotel with their gear bags slung over their shoulders. The key card in hand, Levi opened the door, walked inside, and dropped his bag on the floor near the dresser. Before he could take a breath, Curt slammed him up against the wall with enough force to make him grunt, crushed his mouth against Levi's, and pushed his tongue between Levi's lips. The demanding way he took control, shoved Levi's libido through the ceiling.

He grabbed Curt's shirt in his fists and ripped the middle in two, sending buttons flying in every direction. The warmth of Curt's skin beneath his fingers made them tingle.

Curt pulled his mouth from Levi's before skimming his lips over his jaw, down his neck, reaching his shoulder in the next breath. Through his shirt, Curt bit into his shoulder. The sensation sent desire zinging down his back, straight to his cock.

"Fuck."

"Yeah, we are."

Curt tossed his shirt onto the bed as Levi worked the buttons on his own, so he could pull it off. Curt got his belt off, unbuttoned his pants, and shoved them to the floor.

Within seconds, they both stood naked in front of each other.

"Over the bed and spread those cheeks. I'll get the lube."

Levi bent over the bed, spread his legs, and put one hand on each ass cheek to open his hole for Curt's invasion.

This was going to be fast, furious, and fun. The cold dollop of the lube made his hole contract.

Anticipation had him shivering in need.

Curt positioned his cock with the head against Levi and pushed forcibly until he was totally inside, pelvis to ass.

"I'm gonna ride you hard."

"Good."

Curt pulled out and shoved back in. Sex with him was never boring. They had this connection of loving everything about fucking whether it be hard and fast like this one or slow and methodical like earlier this morning before they left his home. Sweet lovemaking could be good in its own way, but Levi liked this the best.

The sweet burn of penetration eased as the slow build of orgasm took its place. He hoped Curt would allow him to come before he finished himself. He would be in so much pain if he made him wait.

"Oh God."

"Fuck yeah."

The hard pounding drove Levi face first into the bed. Curt fisted his hair as he continued to slam into him at a furious pace. His cock hurt, his balls ached, and he needed to come so badly, he was seeing stars behind his eyes. "I need to come."

"Not yet."

"You're killing me."

"But what a way to die, my friend."

The rough fuck had him moaning his pleasure as he held off his orgasm by biting his lip. When the sensations became too much, he begged, he pleaded, and he cursed the man behind him. "Damn it, Curt. I need to come."

"I'm there, buddy. Come now."

Levi exploded as cum shot over the comforter beneath him. They would have to wash it off, he supposed, but right now he didn't care. Satisfaction rippled through him as Curt jettisoned his own cum into his ass. When Curt shuddered behind him, he knew the other man had found his own pleasure.

The weight of Curt against his back felt like heaven. He liked having the bulk on his. It made him feel like they had a connection no one would be able to break.

As Curt removed his cock, Levi moaned. The loss of the contact left him feeling a little lost.

A hardy slap to his right butt cheek brought him up off the bed as he flipped over onto his back. "What the hell?"

A smile played on Curt's lips. "We need to get moving. I thought you might require a little motivation."

"Motivation for what?"

"A beer and some nachos or something. I'm hungry."

Levi fell back on the bed, his arms out to the sides. "I think I'll stay here and sleep."

"No you won't. We are going out. Get your happy ass up."

"Fine." Levi didn't move.

"Now, buddy."

"What's your hurry?"

"Food."

"All right." Levi stood and reached for his duffle bag with his clean clothes. "I'm going to take a shower first. You might want to wipe the cum from the comforter."

Curt leaned in to kiss him. "One thing."

"What?"

"Remember, you belong to me."

"I do?"

"Yes. As long as we are fucking, we don't dip our stick anywhere besides each other."

Levi kind of liked the possessive look in Curt's gaze and the way he kissed him hard again before slapping him on the ass.

"I need a shower too, so don't be too long."

"I won't."

Once they were both clean and redressed, they headed downstairs and across the parking lot to the bar. When they walked in the place was already wall to wall cowboys and cowgirls. Levi found Butch at a corner table in the back when he waved him over.

"I'll be back in a minute."

"Where you off to?"

"Butch wants to talk to me about something, remember?"

Curt's gaze narrowed. "Remember what I said in the hotel room."

"I won't forget, but no need to worry. I like being exclusive, plus I don't think Butch swings that way."

"Why else would he want to talk to you?" Curt asked, raising his hand to signal the bartender.

"I don't have a clue."

Curt handed him the bottle of beer. Budweiser. The man had been paying attention to his preferences apparently. He tipped the bottle to his lips, letting the malty liquid slide down his throat. It tasted so good, he took another swig before lowering the bottle.

"Did you order food?"

"Not yet."

"Go ahead and order it. I'll go talk to Butch. I won't be gone long."

"Okay."

Levi wandered to the back corner where Butch had a table to himself. "Butch."

"Levi. Thanks for talking with me."

"No problem." Levi sat in the chair next to Butch so they could talk. He knew the other man wanted privacy so they would have to put their heads together to keep the conversation on the down low. "What's up?"

"I wanted to talk to you about—" Butch let the conversation die as one of the other riders stopped at their table.

"Hey, did you two hear Rusty is out for the season?" Chase Wild took the chair across from them.

"Yeah," Levi answered even though he could see the frustration on Butch's face at having their conversation interrupted. "Too bad. I never want to see anyone hurt."

"I know, but that opens the championship up to anyone. He was in first place in the standings. Anyone with a good run over the next few weeks can really make up some ground."

"It sure does, but the cost to Rusty is the end of his season."

"Yeah."

The conversation lagged for a moment. "Will you excuse us, Chase? We were having a private conversation."

"Oh, sorry. I'll mosey on my way then." The other man stood. "Behave yourselves, you two." He laughed like he had a secret neither of the other two knew about.

Whatever. "So, what did you want to say, Butch?"

Butch leaned in. "How do you keep your sexuality a secret so well? I mean, I heard you were gay. Are you?"

"Yes."

"How hard is it to be gay on this circuit?"

"Very difficult. Keeping quite so people aren't uncomfortable with it is the hardest part. I don't want any of the guys to think I'm going to come onto them. I keep my hookups off the circuit." Levi looked into Butch's eyes. "Are you saying you're gay?"

"Yeah, but I don't want people to know. I'm still not comfortable with it. I haven't been with another guy before, just women, but they don't do it for me anymore. I can't get excited with them."

"I've been there myself."

"How do you get past the icky feeling of wanting another man, but afraid to find out he's straight?"

"You have to go to places where other gay men hang out. When I'm on the road, I have a list of places that have gay bars. When everyone else is hanging out at the local honkytonk, I'm usually at a gay bar if I'm in the mood for a hookup. You don't have to worry about figuring out if they are gay there, everyone is."

"Do you have a steady hook up?"

"Yes, but I'm not saying who. I don't think he wants to be out in the open on the circuit, either."

Butch held up his hands. "No problem."

"How did you find out I'm gay?"

"There is a rumor going around that you and Curt are fuck buddies."

"Who told you that?"

"Jefferson."

"I'm going to kill that slimy little bastard."

"It's not true?"

"It doesn't matter if it is or not. Jefferson needs to keep his nose out of my business. He wants Curt himself and he's pissed because Curt and I are rooming together to save on expenses. Curt likes women." It was true, although he didn't say Curt liked men too.

"Well, anyway, it doesn't matter. What you guys do is your own business, no one else's. Behind closed doors, is behind closed doors."

Levi glanced across the bar. Curt stood with his head bent toward a pretty red-head with a straw cowboy hat on.

He seemed engrossed in the conversation, until he looked up and their gazes caught across the bar. Levi could tell Curt was only placating the woman. It was him he wanted.

"Wow," Butch said. "I wish someone would look at me that way."

"What way?" Levi asked, dropping his gaze back to the bottle in his hand.

"The way you just looked at Reese right then."

"Reese?" He knew who he'd been looking at and it wasn't Reese, but when he looked back, he realized Reese stood with his back toward them, leaning on the bar as he nursed a beer, on the other side of the woman Curt was talking to. It might have looked like he was checking out Reese. He figured it was best to let Butch think what he wanted. "Oh, yeah, Reese."

"You really want him, don't you?"

"Yeah, you could say that. Problem is, I don't know which way he swings so I'm letting it go."

"I have it on good authority he likes women."

"Well then, there you go." Levi tipped his bottle to his lips. "By the way, how are you so versed in which way people around here tend to be?"

"I keep my eyes and ears open. If they go after the buckle bunnies, they obviously like women. If they tend to be loners, they could go either way." Butch leaned in. "You, I had pegged from the get go."

"Why's that?"

"You tend to watch the guys and ignore the women. You stay to yourself, but interact with the guys when prompted. You avoid women coming onto you, although you are good to the fans. I saw that woman come onto you last week. You ignored her completely except to be nice."

Damn, I'm going to have to be more careful. "I guess you do have me pegged."

"It's not a bad thing, Levi. I'm very observant, is all. Most of the guys could care less if you're gay or not, from what I hear. There are a couple who avoid you though."

"Yeah, I noticed."

"Jefferson wants Curt."

"You think?"

"Yep. It's written all of his face." He did the chin tip thing guys do when they're trying to get your attention. "He's watching him like a hawk from his spot at the other end of the bar. If you were doing Curt, you'd have a fight on your hands."

"Why do you say that?"

"Because, Jefferson is a fighter. When he wants something, he goes after it."

Levi turned to watch Jefferson and sure enough, he had his gaze focused on Curt. Jealousy surged through him. Curt was his, at least for now. Jefferson could go suck donkey dick. "It really doesn't matter, does it?"

Butch drained his beer. "Nope. I guess not since Curt likes girls."

"Anyway, nice talking to you. I hope you figure out what you want to do."

"I have one more question for you."

"Shoot."

"Would you fuck me?" Butch grasped his cock under the table. "I want someone to initiate me into the world. I think you're hot, Levi, and I would love to have you take me the first time."

Levi squirmed against the hand holding him as he glanced across the bar at Curt. Their gazes met. Curt's eyes narrowed. Levi removed Butch's hand. "Sorry. I'm in a relationship. Things are exclusive so I'm not available."

"Sorry. I didn't know. If you could recommend someone that would be good."

"I'm not sure who, but I'll keep my ears open." Levi stood, grabbed his beer, tipped his hat, and then headed back across the bar toward Curt. He wanted out of here. He'd had his beer and now he wanted the man who made him hard as a rock. Tonight, he wanted on top.

* * * *

Curt watched the scene between Butch and Levi with interest. If he gauged Butch right, the other man had the hots for his guy, which wouldn't do at all. Levi belonged to him, at least for now and until he said otherwise.

When Butch snuck his hand under the table, he saw Levi jump. Good indicator that Butch was coming onto Levi. That wouldn't do at all.

"Curt?"

"Yeah?" he asked absently as he continued to watch the scene.

"I asked you a question."

He glanced back to the woman at his side. "Sorry, I got engrossed in the game on the television against the back wall. I'm a huge football fan." True enough, even if that's not what he'd been watching.

"I asked if you might like to go back to my room. I reserved one for tonight."

"Uh, sorry, babe, but I'm out for tonight. I pulled a groin muscle during my ride. I couldn't fuck right now if my life depended on it." Okay, not true, but he really wasn't into women tonight. The man he wanted had just got up from the table and was headed in his direction. He turned toward the bartender asking about their nachos. They never arrived.

"Sorry, man. I think they were given to someone else. I'll reorder them."

"Thanks."

Levi stopped at his side. "Where's the food?"

"Apparently, they screwed up the order."

"So what? They're coming?"

"Yeah. They are reordering them. They should be here soon."

The red-head turned toward Levi. "Hey, you are kind of cute too. What's your name?"

"Levi."

"I have a room for tonight, Levi. Interested?"

"Sorry, but no."

She glanced between the two of them and then back again. "Oh, I get it. You two are into each other." She waved her finger between them. "That's cool. I think it's hot watching two guys fuck."

"You have it all wrong."

"I don't think so." She got close to Levi's ear, but wasn't the least bit quiet about what she said. "If you two wouldn't mind, I'd love to watch."

Curt leaned his elbow on the bar. "No, really, you are totally mistaken."

The woman smiled knowingly. "Okay. If you say so, but the looks you two are giving each other tell me a totally different story. If you aren't fucking already, you will be soon, because you two are into each other big time."

Their nachos showed up a moment later.

The red-head set her sights on some other cowboy when neither of them responded to her statement. She picked up her beer and headed down the bar, so Levi took her seat.

"These are good for bar food."

"They have a restaurant on the other side of the bar, so they serve all kinds of food, but yeah, these are pretty good."

They ate in silence although Curt could feel the draw of Levi's looks when he glanced in his direction. They would fuck again tonight and he would let Levi have his ass. The heat being sent his way pricked his skin like tiny little darts. Need built slowly inside him. Desire taunted him. He knew what he wanted, but he was going to let the thought of it drive him insane before he gave into the feelings stirring.

"What did Butch want?"

"Besides me?" Levi leaned in to keep his voice down.

"He wanted you to fuck him?"

"Yeah, but he also wanted to know how I handled getting laid without letting all the guys on the circuit know I'm gay." Levi popped another piece of nacho into his mouth, trying not to smile. Levi seemed to be playing on his jealousy a little too much.

"You told him no, right?" Curt asked, hoping that he wouldn't have to kill Butch for trying to take what was his and his alone.

"No, to what, getting laid or by him?"

"By him."

"Of course, I told him no. We said we were exclusive."

His breath whooshed out in relief. "Good."

"I don't fuck around, Curt. Never have."

"I'm glad to hear that."

"Jealous someone else wants me?"

"Hell yeah, I'm jealous. I'll say it. I'm the jealous sort. Get used to it."

"Someone on this circuit wants you too. Should I be jealous?"

"Who?" he asked, his gaze zipping around the room as he tried to figure out who might be wanting to get in his jeans.

"Jefferson."

"That little weasel? Hell no."

"What about the woman?"

"I told her no too. I said I pulled a groin muscle riding tonight so I was out of commission."

"You lied?"

"Yes, I wasn't about to tell her I was fucking you although I think she had us pegged."

"Yeah, I think so."

They finished up the nachos and drank the last dregs of their beers. "You ready to call it a night?"

Levi stood as he pushed his beer bottle to toward the bartender. "Yep. I'm going to need to hit the gym in the hotel in the morning to work out the muscles in my arms. My shoulder is a bit sore tonight."

"What time do we need to be at the arena tomorrow?"

"The event starts at six. We should be done by ten."

They walked out of the bar, headed for Levi's truck. The night air had gotten cooler, bringing up goose bumps on his skin since he hadn't worn a jacket, just his long-sleeved shirt. "Cool…early enough to get some shut-eye and then head to the next one." He opened the door on the passenger side as soon as Levi clicked the button. "Where do we go from here?"

"South Dakota."

"That's what? Another ten hour drive?"

"Twelve. It's pretty straight forward from here. We can spend more time at the ranch before we head up there if we leave Monday morning. Next weekend is a three day event though, so we can stay at the ranch until Thursday, drive up that morning, spend the night near the venue, and be there for the event Friday. I think the first day starts at two."

"Sounds good."

Within a couple of minutes, they were back in their room. "Are you going to fuck me or what?"

Chapter Eleven

Levi walked with a little strut in his step as they made their way to the arena the next day. He could proudly say he made Curt lose his cool the night before when he fucked him to the point of speechlessness. He made sure to wind him up until he was ready to explode and then Levi made him hold off on his orgasm. He stroked him slow, then fast, then slow again. The rub of his cock in and out of Curt's ass drove him crazy.

"You are walking like a peacock with its feathers fanned today, Levi."

"I have a right to. You were almost babbling last night."

"I was not," Curt replied, although a smile played on his lips. He glanced around the backroom where they were standing for a minute before reaching in to kiss Levi on the mouth. "It was awesome. I'm certainly not complaining."

"Good."

They both grabbed their bull ropes and their chaps before heading out to the area behind the chutes. After they wrapped them around the metal railing, they worked the rosin into the material of the rope, making sure the part they gripped in their hand was as sticky as they could make it. Levi noticed Curt's rope was frayed at the end.

"You need a new rope."

"Yeah, this one is a bit rough."

"You shouldn't use it with that on the end. If you hang up your spur, you could get killed."

"I don't have another rope."

"You don't have a spare?"

"Nope."

Levi grabbed his spare from his bag. "Here. Use mine."

"No. This one has brought me luck. I can't change now."

Levi shrugged. "Suit yourself."

Soon, the announcers were introducing all the riders. They did their walk out to the middle of the arena, up on the shark tank, and then back down as the next rider came up. It was the same every weekend, although the lineup changed with each event.

As the riders got ready behind the chutes, the first to go were those whose scores were the lowest on the leaderboard. Curt would go second to the last, with Levi riding last since he was in first place overall.

All the riders did well. Everyone managed to stay on their bull for the full eight.

Next up was Curt.

Levi got up on the chute with him as Curt worked himself onto the back of his bull. This one would be tough, not like they all weren't tough, but this particular bull liked to spin as he bucked. He was one of the most difficult bulls to ride on the circuit for a lefty like Curt.

Once Curt was prepped, he pulled the rope around his fist and then back across his palm. The nod of his head was miniscule, but it was there nonetheless as the gatekeeper opened the chute.

The ride seemed to be going fine, and then all of the sudden his spur caught in the flank strap around the back of the bull as he tried to dismount. The bull continued to buck. One hoof caught Curt in the side of the head. The strap broke on his helmet, sending the safety gear flying clear. Curt continued to bounce around until the bull fighters could manage to reach up with a knife and cut the spur loose from the rope. In the process, Curt took another blow to the head.

When they finally got him loose, he was unconscious on the arena floor.

Levi's heart dropped into his stomach as he gripped the railing beneath his hands with a white-knuckled grip. He wanted to rush out there to see to his lover, but he couldn't even if they would allow him to.

The medical doctor in charge of riders rushed out with the team of medical personal to see to Curt. He hadn't moved.

Time stopped as Levi waited with bated breath. *He has to be okay. He can't be hurt really badly. I don't know what I'll do if he is. I need him.*

The crowd was silent. Nothing moved as they all waited for some sign Curt Walsh would be okay.

The medical team moved him onto the gurney, lifted him into the air and rushed him through the exit chute, back through the throng of riders, and down the hall to the waiting room set aside for medical issues.

Levi couldn't go. He had to ride. He was up next.

He managed to switch chutes where his bull waited, impatiently banging his horns on the railings. Levi got into position although his mind was on Curt, and not on his ride. *I need to focus.*

"Word has it folks, Curt Walsh will be okay. He's conscious now although he appears to have a concussion."

The crowd roared with approval and Levi could relax just a little. At least he knew Curt was awake.

Levi nodded for the gatekeeper to release the chute.

Time froze. Lights whirled as he did his damndest to stay centered on the bull. His butt spun around in circles.

The bull changed positioned, first twirling to the right, then switching it up and spinning to the left.

The buzzer sounded.

He released his hand from the rope and jumped clear of the bull, rushing for the fence to avoid being gored.

The bull fighters corralled the bull, chasing him out of the arena.

Levi could breathe again as he grabbed his bull rope from them before heading back behind the chutes.

He glanced up at the score board. He'd done well, but didn't win the event, although he took second and his rankings in the world championship run probably went up by at least five spots. Curt would qualify now with his standing. One of the late qualifiers from the day before who'd ridden both of the bulls yesterday, and finished strong today, won the event by a mere half point. Cody Nash was a good rider. He was hanging in there in the race for the finals too.

Chaps swishing around his legs, he walked back to the locker room to remove his gear. He would check on Curt in a minute. He didn't want to seem too anxious to find out about his lover's condition. He might give away their relationship if he did.

He worked on his chaps' buckles next to his gear bag in the corner. Once he had them loose he pushed the leather free of his body and stepped out. Taking the time to roll the chaps carefully, he slipped them along with his bull rope in his bag, zipped it up and pushed the whole kit toward the wall.

He inhaled a cleansing breath as he adjusted the hat on his head. Calm, he needed to be calm in the face of his lover's injury. Going in there freaking out because of blood, wouldn't be the best thing.

"Levi?" someone called.

"Yeah?"

"Curt is asking for you."

"Be right there." With a quickness to his step, he walked through the doorway, out in the hall and into the next room.

Curt was lying on a gurney with a bandage wrapped around his head. There was blood clinging to the white dressing.

"Levi!"

"I'm right here," he said, moving to Curt's side.

His lover looked pale and drawn. "There you are. Where have you been?"

"Getting my gear put away."

"Your gear is more important than me?"

"No." He glanced around. The doctor and his assistant stood near a desk where they were talking softly, ignoring the conversation going on between him and Curt. "I couldn't make it seem obvious."

"What?"

"Our relationship."

"Who cares? I don't. If the whole damned circuit knows we're fucking, it's our business."

"Keep your voice down."

"I won't. I want everyone to know. I'm done hiding behind a mask of indifference. I like fucking men. I like fucking women. What the hell does it matter to anyone?"

The doctor looked over in their direction with a raised eyebrow.

"Sshh."

"I will not. I fucking love you, man."

Levi knew it was the concussion talking, not the Curt he knew. Curt would never say something like that with others around. "I love you too. We are great friends, but you need to rest now. You've got a bad concussion." He glanced at the doctor, who nodded in understanding. Hopefully, they dodged a bullet.

"No worries, Levi. He's been talking crazy ever since we brought him back here. We know he's not making sense."

"Thanks, Doc."

"Besides, even if you two are a couple, it's okay with us."

"We've traveling partners and friends. That's it."

"Okay. Whatever. I just wanted to let you know, no skin off our noses here. What you two do in your hotel room is your own business."

"What do I need to do, Doc?"

"You can take him back to your room. Watch him tonight. If he has a seizure or gets sick to his stomach, call 911."

"A seizure?"

"Yeah. He has a pretty good concussion, but I've seen worse. He'll be okay. Wake him every couple of hours to make sure he wakes up easily, otherwise, let him sleep. He should be more aware tomorrow morning. He probably won't remember anything about the last day or two. Concussions typically do that."

"Okay." Levi helped Curt sit up. "We need to get his chaps off."

"I'll help you." The doctor's assistant moved over to help Levi work the chaps off Curt's ass and thighs.

By the time they had them off, Curt was sitting glassy eyed on the gurney.

"I'll be right back. Let me throw his stuff in his bag, grab our gear, and take it to my truck." Levi stopped at the door. "Will he be okay to ride next week?"

"He should be fine."

"Okay. Thanks, Doc."

"Sure."

Levi got their stuff together, put it in his vehicle, and then headed back into pick up his partner.

Curt sat on the gurney with the help of the doctor. "Is he going to be okay to walk to the truck and into the hotel with me?"

"He might be a little wobbly, but you should be okay. If you want, one of us can go over there with you to help you get him settled."

"That would be great."

"Tom, will you help Levi? I've got this here and we are done for the night."

"Sure."

The hotel was next door to the arena, so the assistant would be able to walk back. Levi was grateful for the help.

They no sooner got him into the hotel room, and he started snoring in the bed.

"Wake him in a couple of hours. He should be fine until then."

"Thanks, Tom. I appreciate the help and the reassurance. I haven't had to deal with someone who had a head injury before."

"It's not a bad one. Like Doc said, he's seen worse. The hoof glanced off his skull. He probably got the head injury more from being bounced around by his spur, than anything."

He clapped Tom on the shoulder. "You guys are the best."

"It's our job." He walked toward the door. "I hope you can get a little sleep tonight, but don't worry about him. He'll be okay."

"Thanks again."

"You're welcome."

After the door shut behind Tom, Levi tossed his hat into the chair and raked his fingers through his hair. *I really could use a beer, but yeah, that's out.*

Curt softly snored from the bed, leaving Levi to entertain himself for the evening. Oh well. It was kind of late anyway and they had two beds in the room, so he could sleep in the other one without any difficulty. The bad part would be waking Curt every couple of hours. He'd have to set an alarm. At least tomorrow, they would be headed back to his ranch and Curt could recuperate there for the next few days by sitting around, eating Emma's cooking, watching television or whatever else he wanted to do. No work for him.

The chair looked comfortable enough to check his email and call his parents. He wanted to let them know they would be back at the ranch tomorrow. He really needed to get in touch with his publicity guy so they could work on setting up some personal engagements. Those kinds of things were important to his career. He wanted to be the fan favorite going into the finals.

He grabbed his cell phone to call his mom.

"Hey, Mom," he said, when she answered.

"Hey, baby. You did good this weekend again. Your dad and I watched it on the television."

"Thanks. I didn't win, but the points will help me."

"That's great, Levi." There was a pause on the line. "How is Curt? He looked like he'd been hurt pretty badly after his ride."

"He's fine. Concussion and some scrapes from being thrown around. He got his spur caught in the flank strap. The doctor said he'll be fine. He's sleeping in the bed next to me right now, snoring."

"Should he be sleeping? I thought they wanted you to keep people awake who had concussions."

"Not anymore. Doc said he could sleep, but to wake him every couple of hours. The main thing is to watch for seizures or throwing up. They seemed to think he only got a glancing blow from the bull, the concussion came from being whipping around."

"I'm glad he'll be okay."

"Yeah, me too." He switched the phone to his other ear. "I wanted to let you know we'll be back at the ranch tomorrow for a couple of days. Our next stop is South Dakota so we can spend a few days at home."

"Wonderful! You two will have to come over for supper again."

"Of course, Mom. We wouldn't have it any other way."

"Good."

He wanted to tell his mom how worried he was about Curt after he'd been hurt, but he held back. The thought of having feelings for the other man scared the hell out of him, but there it was.

The sick feeling he'd had when Curt got hung up stayed with him. Terror at the thought of losing his lover had him almost throwing up himself. What would happen if Curt had been really hurt? How would he feel? What if he'd died?

The thought terrified him.

"Levi?"

"Yeah, Mom?"

"Are you okay, son?"

"I'm not sure."

"Talk to me, honey. You know I'm here to help you."

"I know, but I'm not sure where to start."

"How about at the beginning? When did you realize you were falling in love with Curt?"

"Am I?"

"I think so."

"I can't though, Mom. He doesn't want a permanent relationship. We are lovers, nothing more. If I try to bring feelings into this, I'm afraid I'll lose him for good."

"I don't think so, Levi. I saw the way he watched you while you two were here. I think he has feelings for you too, although he might not want to admit it just yet."

Levi blew out a heavy breath. "What am I going to do?"

"Play it by ear, baby. He'll come around when the time is right." He could hear the smile in her voice. "I think you two are cute together, but be cautious. Don't push. He seems skittish about having a long-term relationship with another man. I know you aren't like that, so I think you'll do fine, but he's not as comfortable with it."

"Thanks, Mom." His heart swelled with love for his mother and her understanding.

"You're welcome. So we'll see you tomorrow for supper?"

"Let's make it Tuesday so Curt has time to just chill out at the house for a day. I don't know how long he'll be confused after he wakes up in the morning. He might be perfectly fine, but there is still the chance he could have some muddled brain stuff going on."

"No problem. We'll plan on Tuesday then."

"I love you."

"Love you too, son. See you later and be careful driving home."

"Bye, Mom." Levi hung up the phone, putting it down on the small table next to his chair. Curt continued to snore softly from the bed across the room. What to do? He really wasn't sure. He knew feelings were coming in to the situation, at least on his part, but did Curt have any feelings for him at all? He wasn't sure and how to approach the subject with his lover was another thing on his mind.

He should probably get some shut-eye since he had to set an alarm to wake Curt every couple of hours. It was going to be a long night.

The next morning Levi rolled over with a groan. He felt like shit after only getting a few hours of sleep. Luckily the every two hours waking schedule for Curt went well. Curt had been coherent for the most part the later the wakings became. He was able to answers questions about where they were, what had happened, who he was, what day it was, and the most important part to Levi was who his lover was.

It would feel good to be in his own bed tonight.

Curt woke himself a few minutes later. "God, I feel like I've been kicked by a bull."

"You were, slick."

"Well hell, no wonder my head hurts." Curt touched the bandage on his head. "I don't remember much."

"I bet you don't. You had a pretty good concussion. Thank God for your helmet, otherwise you would have taken a direct blow to the head."

"What happened?"

"Your spur hooked in the flank strap. You were thrown around like a ragdoll for a minute before the bull fighters cut you loose. The bull got a kick off to your helmet. The strap broke and it went flying. The second one glanced off your skull, thus the bandage and concussion. Doc says you'll be fine, but you were out cold for a few minutes and you've been confused most of the night."

"Did I at least win?"

"No, but you came in third. Cody Nash took the final win."

"Good for him. Points?"

"You gained enough to qualify. Now you just have to hang on and keep riding well to make the finals."

A groan escaped Curt's lips as he sat up on the side of the bed. "How did I get back here?"

"I brought you back from the emergency room with instructions to wake you every two hours. You've been doing fine during the night, but I imagine things will be clearer today."

"What's the plan?"

"Head to my place to rest up for a couple of days. You okay to drive?"

"I think so. My eyes aren't crossing and my vision is clear. I have a headache though. A couple of Tylenol would be great right now."

Levi climbed to his feet to fetch the pills from his bag. He always kept some on hand because of the regular muscle aches and pains he had during the circuit regular events. After he shook out a couple into his hand, he retrieved a glass of water, and then walked to Curt's side. "Here you go."

"Thanks. If I didn't feel like shit right now, I'd kiss you."

"We'll save it for later."

Curt peeled one eye opened and looked up. "I appreciate you taking care of me. I don't know what I would have done without you."

"Probably fallen on your ass and been fucked by Jefferson."

"Oh hell no!"

Levi grinned. He liked teasing Curt with the threat of the other man fucking him. Jefferson wasn't the best option for a man on man thing. The guy was a jerk and Levi couldn't see Curt giving him the time of day, but you never know. Things could change between him and Curt in a heartbeat. He hoped they didn't. He loved having Curt around. "Shall we get moving? I'd like to be at the ranch before lunch. You can rest this afternoon if you want. The sunlight on the way home might hurt your head some."

"Okay." Curt stood, swaying a little on his feet as he adjusted to the height difference.

"Are you sure you'll be able to drive?"

"Do I have a choice? I can't leave my truck here."

"True. I'll keep an eye on you in my rearview mirror. If I see you swerving or anything, we'll leave your vehicle somewhere on the way. It's not that far to come back and get it if we need to."

"Sounds good."

"I'll grab your gear."

Curt's lips twisted into a small grin. "Let me take a piss before we leave. My bladder feels like it's about to explode."

"I'll take the gear down. Where are your keys?"

"In my pants pocket." He reached in the left front pocket of his jeans. "I would have you go after them, but I'm really not up to extracurricular activity at the moment." Dangling them from his fingers, he said, "I'll take a kiss though."

Levi couldn't resist the wry grin on Curt's mouth, so he leaned in and plastered his lips against Curt's. A groan escaped his mouth as Curt pushed his tongue between Levi's lips and deep into his mouth. Would he ever be able to get enough of this man? He was beginning to think the impossible. He was in love with Curt Walsh.

Chapter Twelve

Curt's head felt like it was splitting in two. The sunlight burned right through his sunglasses to pierce his eyes like someone was stabbing him with a fork. God, it hurt to breathe. He'd make it though, he had to. He could rest when they got to Levi's, thank goodness. He needed to sleep or something. The Tylenol didn't seem to do much for the headache. He had something stronger in his bag from past breaks, sprains, and other various ailments he'd acquired over the last few years. A couple of Loratab would help.

A few minutes later, they pulled down the dirt road to Levi's ranch. The bumping along didn't help the pain in his head, but it would be over soon.

The house came into view. He really liked the older farmhouse with its shutters and porch. It reminded him of his grandparents place from so long ago. He hadn't been there in years, but this had the same feel. Home.

As they stopped their vehicles in front, he slowly climbed out of his truck with a groan. His whole body hurt from being tossed around, his leg especially after being caught. It was his fault. He should have checked the flank strap, he supposed, although it was the contractors responsibility to make sure they weren't frayed. He didn't know if that was what his spur caught in or not this time. It wouldn't happen again. He'd make damn sure there wasn't anything to screw up his ride again.

"Come on. Let's get you into bed."

"I told you I wasn't up for fucking today, Levi." He grinned.

Levi shook his head. "Tomorrow."

"I'll be up for tomorrow, maybe. I need to take something stronger than Tylenol and sleep for a couple of hours."

They walked through the front door, expecting a squeal from Emma. When it didn't arrive, they turned to look at each other.

"I wonder where Emma is."

Curt glanced into the kitchen, finding it empty and silent.

The front door opened and closed. Nick poked his head around the doorframe. "Where's Emma?"

"I don't know. We just got here."

"This isn't like her. She didn't fix breakfast this morning either."

"I'll run to her house after I get Curt settled to check on her. I'm worried now." Levi ushered him inside and up the stairs to his bedroom. "You climb up there. Where are the Loratab?"

"In my gear bag."

"I'll get them. Close your eyes and rest."

"I hope everything is okay with Emma."

"Me too. It's not like her to miss work. She must be really sick."

Levi disappeared out the door as he closed his eyes, willing the headache to dissipate. The pounding in his skull felt like someone was stabbing him in the forehead with something sharp right through his eye.

A moment later, Levi returned with the pills and a glass of water. "Here. Take these."

Curt sat up, took the medication from Levi's hand and swallowed the two pills before lying back down on the soft pillows. He let the feathers envelope his head, cushioning him as he rested. Levi brushed his lips over his before Curt heard the soft click of the door as he left.

Two hours later, he awoke to the smell of food being cooked in the kitchen. His head no longer hurt and his thoughts were clear when he sat up on the side of the bed. His stomach rumbled. They hadn't eaten breakfast before they'd made the trek to Levi's place this morning.

Levi pushed open the door with his foot as he came inside with a tray in hand. "You're up. Good. I brought food. I hope you like BLTs."

"I love them," he said, reaching for the tray. "Did you find Emma?"

"Yeah. She is sick as a dog with the flu. I called my mom who came over to help nurse her. She hadn't eaten since yesterday, had been throwing up the night before, and running a fever. I told Mom I would check on her this afternoon and bring her something to eat if Mom needed to leave. She assured me my dad could function without her for supper tonight."

Curt bit into the sandwich. "This is good. You aren't bad in the kitchen, huh?"

Levi shrugged as he sat down on the bed. "I can manage a few things, but don't expect me to make an elaborate meal. I'm no chef."

"Did you eat already?"

"Yeah, I ate with the ranch hands while you slept." He brushed his hand through Curt's hair at the nap of his neck. "Do you feel better? You look better."

"I feel a hundred percent better. Sleeping and the medication helped tremendously. The headache is gone."

"Great! I'm glad to hear it." Levi fell silent for a moment as he crossed and recrossed his boots at the ankle.

"Are you feeling up to working on the books this afternoon while I work in the barn?"

"If you want me to, or I could help you in the barn." Curt waggled his eyebrows. "I'm sure the tack room needs straightening up, right?"

"You shouldn't be pushing yourself today, I imagine."

"Let me decide what I feel like doing, okay? You don't need to babysit me anymore. I'm fine."

"Sorry. I care, Curt. I can't help it. I don't want to see you down in pain again this evening."

Curt's heart did a little wiggle in his chest. *Levi cared?* "No need to worry. I'll be okay. This isn't the worse thing to happen to a bull rider."

"I know that, of course."

"Then ease up."

"Do what you want then. Just don't blame me when you can't function later."

"I'll be able to function just fine in more ways than one. I should take advantage of this pain free moment." He glanced down at Levi's crotch, letting his gaze take in Levi's lack of hard-on. Maybe his lover was getting tired of him. Maybe it was time to move on. "I'll do the books if you'd rather."

"I just figured you shouldn't be doing anything strenuous like shoveling horse shit."

"Or fucking you until you are babbling like an idiot?"

"That too."

Curt growled as he pulled Levi so their mouths almost touched. "Fine. I'll give in this one time, but don't get used to it. I'm rather used to being the dominant one in the relationship."

Levi grinned as he locked his gaze on Curt's. "I know. It's one of the things I like about you."

He brushed his lips against Levi's. "Be prepared for me later. I want you to make love to me." *Make love? Where the hell did that come from?* "You know what I mean."

"Yes, I certainly do."

Levi picked up the tray and disappeared out the door as Curt stood. His head didn't swim, thank goodness, and there were no residual effects from the pounding he took in the arena the day before. He took a gander at his clothes. They were dirty and dusty. He should never have slept on Levi's bed in them, but he hadn't felt very good earlier.

Dirt clung to the coverlet. He'd throw it and the sheets in the washer after Levi went outside to work. It was the least he could do for the care Levi had given him while he'd been down. He would have to thank him properly tonight with a good blow job. Those always made things better.

The screen banged shut as Levi went outside. Curt looked out the window, watching Levi saunter across the grass toward the barn. Once he disappeared inside the huge double doors, Curt grabbed the comforter and sheets off the bed and took them downstairs with him. He would take a quick shower once he had them in the laundry.

The laundry room sat off the kitchen. He would wash the comforter alone and then the sheets. It would be nice to have freshly washed linens on the bed when they made love tonight.

There's it was again. Made love. Is that really how I feel about fucking Levi? His thoughts drifted to their last time together. It really had been fucking that time, but he kind of liked the idea of making love to Levi. Tender, passionate, love was something he wasn't used to in a relationship, but he figured it was worth a shot. It couldn't be any worse than the reaming they had done in the past. He liked it both ways.

After Curt had the comforter in the washer, he turned it on and made his way to Levi's bathroom to shower and change clothes before he started on the books in Levi's office.

Once he was dressed, he headed for the room off the living room, where Levi did his business. He liked the space. Brown leather seemed to be a theme with his lover. The couch had quality brown leather coverings as did the matching chairs. The desk was mahogany with leather inserts covering the space where you work. Dark curtains hung over the windows, blocking out the sunlight, and keeping the space mysterious. Two big books shelves lined one wall with several bound novels, gracing the space. Levi was well read if the selection of reading material said anything.

Curt grabbed the large ledgers Levi used to keep track of his expenses and income. Scanning the numbers, Curt began to do some figuring on the calculator to his right. The books looked good. Levi had a steady income from selling off his beef cattle and raising his horses, but he also was doing fairly well with his income from bull riding. Not that the ranch wasn't self-sufficient, but he figured Levi's money from the circuit helped with expenses. If he retired from bull riding in the next couple of years, Levi would be comfortable with his money, no doubt.

Investments were doing well too. He needed to dig a little more to find out just how well, but it appeared he didn't have to worry about money.

The numbers looked great. He would be able to tell Levi the good news when they had supper that night.

Supper.

Hmm. He could probably whip something up for everyone to eat depending on what Emma had in the house. He would have to check the kitchen in a little bit to see what there might be to make.

He did a few more adjustments to the books that didn't take too long at all considering Levi was really bad about receipts and marking what was personal items verses business expenses. He would have to talk to Levi about that. Maybe he should just take over doing the books all together. That would mean some kind of commitment on his part to this thing with Levi. Was he ready for that?

Hell, if I know. I like the thought of being around Levi all the time, but am I willing to promise to be in an exclusive relationship with him? "Yeah, I kind of am." Man, he wished he had someone to talk to about this, but he really didn't. Maybe he could talk to Levi's mom. She understood their kind of relationship and she might be able to give him some advice.

Levi had mentioned they were going over to his parents' place for supper tomorrow evening. If he could get a couple of minutes alone with her, he would ask her opinion. Too bad he couldn't talk to his own mother. She would flip out.

Tonight would be a night alone, just the two of them. They could sit and watch a movie, hang out, or do whatever. He liked those kinds of evenings and they didn't get to do it much on the circuit. It was always traveling from one place to another, meet and greets with fans, riding, then moving onto the next venue. Breaks were far and few between in this life, but it was the life they both chose when they began their bull riding career. You took the good with the bad.

Curt closed the book and headed to the kitchen. When he opened the door to the refrigerator, he found Emma had taken out beef tips. He could do something with that, he figured, if she had noodles and some sauce mix. Beef and noodles always filled a bunch of hungry men.

Before he knew it, the screen banged shut as the men started filing in. "What smells so good?" Nick said, stopping near the doorframe.

"Beef tips and noodles."

"One of my favorites," one of the other hands remarked.

"Good. Take a seat and I'll dish it up."

Levi stopped next to him. "You didn't have to cook. We could have ordered pizza or something for supper."

"I wanted to. It's the least I could do for everything you did for me over the last couple of days." Curt knew the ranch hands were aware of their boss' sexual preferences, but he wasn't sure if Levi wanted it to be in their face with personal displays of affection, so he held off touching, or kissing Levi in front of them until he knew for sure."I didn't do anything."

"Yes you did. You've been babysitting me, making sure I didn't do anything stupid while I was out of my mind."

"All right, you two. Knock off the kissy face shit. Let's eat. I'm starving," Nick said, with a laugh as the other hands all took seats around the table.

Curt laughed. *I guess they wouldn't be bothered by us displaying affection for one another other than like a sibling making gagging sounds.* He served each man in turn with a large plate of the food along with a couple of slices of bread to help fill out the meal.

By the time supper was over, each man had cleaned their plates twice. Luckily, he'd fixed a lot of food knowing the way men eat.

"You won't be replacing Emma, but you make some damned good chow." Victor slapped him on the back. "Glad to have you around, Curt. I hope you'll be staying for a while." Victor winked at him before he took his leave, followed by the rest of the hands.

Levi rinsed the plates in the sink and stacked them in the dishwasher to be run through shortly. "Supper was great, Curt. You're a pretty good cook. Better than me. I can only do simple things."

"It wasn't anything special, but I like to cook. I hung out a lot in the kitchen when I was a kid helping the cook out while Mom and Dad were off doing their thing. She watched us as well as being the cook. My sister didn't like the domestic goddess thing, so she bestowed her knowledge on me while I sat on a barstool listening to her sing. She had a beautiful voice."

"What was her name?"

"Esperanza. She was a Mexican woman. Her husband worked the ranch with my dad. They raised their kids on my parents place until they all moved on with their own lives."

"Is she still there?"

"Yes, but now she has grandkids running around the ranch. Her husband doesn't wrangle anymore, but he helps Dad with the cattle birthings and such."

When the kitchen had been cleaned, they moved into the living room to take a seat on the couch. "I need to make a trip over to Rachel's to check on her and my nephew. Do you want to go?"

"That sounds great."

"Want to watch a movie after we get back?"

"Sure."

Two hours later, they arrived back at the ranch. The visit with Levi's sister was great. She looked amazing for just given birth. The baby was cute as babies go, although he wasn't sure about holding them, even though she thrust the wiggling infant into his arms for a few minutes. Luckily, the little boy didn't cry or anything. He could handle one under those terms. It would be interesting when or if he finally became a dad. He wanted kids, sure, but it might be a long time if ever before he had any.

Levi picked out something from the vast collection he had along the wall, popped it into the DVD player, grabbed the remote, and then sat back down on the couch next to him. "I grabbed an action flick."

"Sounds good."

They sat side-by-side watching Fast and Furious on the huge television in Levi's living room. Well, Levi watched as Curt watched Levi.

"Do I have something on my face?"

"No, why?"

"You keep looking at me."

"Just not interested in the movie, I guess. I'm more interested in you."

Levi turned to look at him. "Why is that?"

"Because I'm horny as hell and I can't wait for this movie to be over."

Levi touched his chest with the palm of his hand. "Why didn't you say so?"

"Because you wanted to watch the movie." He grabbed Levi's hand, pushing it down his abdomen to his crotch. "I'm not hard for one of the ranch hands."

"Wanna fuck out here or in the bedroom?"

"I think I'd like you to take me over the arm of the couch."

"I'll get the lube."

Levi disappeared up the stairs as fast as lightning flashing across the sky while Curt grinned. The enthusiasm of his lover never ceased to amaze him. Curt heard the drawer open, then close in the upstairs bedroom while he unbuckled his belt, slipped off his shirt, and unbuttoned his jeans, leaving them open at the waist. He wanted Levi to remove the Wranglers in a slow push off his hips. He loved it when his lover undressed him. The look in his eyes always mesmerized him with their heavy sexual desire.

Breathless, Levi skidded to a halt in his socks and nothing else. His cock bobbed against his abdomen in a dance as old as time. Pre-cum glistened on the end of his penis.

"I'm ready. Why aren't you undressed?"

"I wanted you to take them off."

"Stand up."

"I need to do something first." Curt took the end of Levi's cock in his mouth, tasting the salty liquid on the pad of his tongue.

Levi moaned as he rocked his hips closer, fisting his hands in Curt's hair. "So good."

The hard flesh slid along his tongue to the back of his throat. He closed his lips around Levi's cock. He loved the feeling of having Levi's entire length in his mouth, tonguing the veins that ran the length of his flesh, and bringing his lover to his knees with pleasurable sensations.

"Curt?"

"Yeah?" he responded, letting Levi's cock pop from his mouth.

"I want to be inside you more than anything."

"Come and get me, babe."

He stood and Levi tugged at his jeans near his hips, pushing the soft material down over his buttocks, and past his thighs. Levi wrapped a hand around his cock, taking the thick rod in his mouth for a few minutes before he helped him work his jeans off his feet.

Levi turned him around and pushed him with a hand in the middle of his back. "Bend over the arm there. Spread those cheeks for me. I want to see that hole."

Dirty talk always turned him on. "Fuck yeah." The dollop of cold liquid hit his ass making him suck in a ragged breath. He didn't need any priming this time. He was fully erect and ready to blow at any second.

The hard head of Levi's cock pressed against his ass, slowly penetrating the ring of muscles at his anus. The sweet burn left him shivering. The fullness of the penetration gave him the sensation of needing to push back against Levi's invasion.

When he felt Levi's pubic hair against his ass, he sighed at the feeling of completeness, of oneness, and of the love he felt.

Love? Oh shit!

* * * *

Levi sighed as he pushed inside Curt. The soft slide of his cock into Curt's ass gave him goose bumps up and down his body. The tight grip of the anal passage made him want to pound his cock into his lover with a fierceness of possession he didn't know he had.

Mine.

"Faster, Levi. Fuck me harder."

Not willing to waste their time together, Levi began a steady pace that increased in intensity twofold with every thrust. He gave as good as he got in this relationship, and he wanted Curt to enjoy their lovemaking as much as he did.

His thrusting became uncoordinated as he got closer and closer to reaching his climax. Curt's breath came out in a seesawing motion beneath him, so Levi knew he was close too. "Come on, Curt. Let go. Come for me."

As Curt lost the tenuous hold on his orgasm, Levi's disappeared too. He came hard in Curt's ass, spurting cum out the end of his dick in long, agonizing streams of hot liquid that made his balls hurt and his dick ache. He shuddered as he leaned over Curt's back, collapsing them both against the hard surface of the arm of the couch.

"Holy mother of God."

"Yeah."

Levi withdrew his softening cock and stepped back. "I need a shower. Care to join me?"

"Hell yeah. It's my turn to fuck you."

"Let's go then."

A deep joyful laughter rumbled through him, as Levi sprinted back up the stairs to his bedroom and through the bathroom door. Curt was right on his heels as he turned on the hot water, letting the spray warm the room. He glanced around to make sure there were towels available before he jumped into the open shower stall. Curt climbed in right behind him. The multiple directional sprays of water splashed on different parts of his body, massaging the tired muscles of his day of labor. He probably should have taken one when he came in from working, but supper had been ready, and then they got busy doing other things. "Sorry about the sweat."

The rough pad of Curt's tongue did a little dance from his shoulder to his left nipple. "It tastes good on you."

"You're just saying that."

"Nope. I like sweaty flesh on my tongue. It reminds me there are hardworking people out there." Curt stepped closer to run a hand down Levi's chest. "You are built hard, just like I enjoy it. Rough, strong, and muscular are my favorite types."

Levi groaned as Curt's hand encircled his fully erect cock. *Damn. I've never been as horny in my entire life as I am around him.*

"Are you horny, lover?"

"Hell yes. You make me so hot, I can't stand it."

"Good, because I'm hard for you too. You wind me up so tight, I could explode enough to shoot out the tiles in this fantastic shower."

Curt's hand continued to caress his cock as Levi moaned his satisfaction at the sensations zipping through him. Pleasure, pain, and desire warred with each other as he tried to process each one. Basking in the need rocking his body, he braced his hands on the side of the shower stall. "Fuck me."

"Oh, I plan to. In a minute though. I'm going to make you so horny, you will detonate the minute I'm inside your ass."

"Shit."

Curt's hands danced down Levi's back, caressing the globes of his ass with both hands, kneading and sliding his palms along the skin. "Oh yeah. You are so solid. I love running my hands over your muscles." He kept going, down the backs of Levi's thighs, massaging the flesh in the process. It felt heavenly to his tired muscles. "Turn around."

Levi turned, bracing his back against the cold tile of the shower as Curt's mouth encircled his cockhead. His tongue licked from Levi's balls to the tip of his cock, licking around and around the head as Curt rolled Levi's balls with his hands. He thought he would die with the need to come. His nuts ached, drawing up tight against his body. "Please."

"Please what?"

"Fuck me."

After a final lick from balls to head, Curt spun him around, bent him at the waist, and positioned his cock at the entrance to Levi's ass.

"Lube?"

"Where?"

"In the drawer next to the shower."

"Hang tight. Don't move."

The drawer opened and then closed as Curt retrieved the lube tube out of the vanity.

With his eyes closed, Levi relished the desire rushing through him to feel Curt's cock in his ass again. Would he ever get enough of this? He didn't think so, which is why he knew he was in love with Curt and wanted to spend the rest of his life with him. Did Curt feel the same? He wasn't sure. They really needed to talk, but not right now. Right now, he had a need and he was dying to have it fulfilled by the hard flesh of his lover.

"You're so hot standing there like that, waiting for me with your ass positioned just right for my cock."

"Hurry."

"I plan to take this slow."

"Fuck."

"Oh yeah. I do plan to fuck you in a second, but it's going to be a slow ride. I want to enjoy being in your ass."

The next thing Levi felt was the piercing on Curt's cock as he slid his hard flesh into his ass. He couldn't put the feeling into words any more than he could form coherent sounds at the moment.

Slow.

God, Curt was going to kill him with this pace. "Harder. Faster."

"Nope. I'm driving this bus. Enjoy. That's all you have to do."

In. Out. In. Out. He was going to die, sure as shit, he was going to die before he was able to come.

Curt leaned over his back. "Grab your cock and stroke it while I fuck you."

Holy hell.

"Oh my God. Please. Can I come?"

Curt increased the pace of his thrusts until he was pounding into Levi's ass with a force strong enough to push him against the tiles. "Come now, Levi. Give me everything you've got."

Levi came hard, harder than he'd ever come before in his life, as cum painted the tiles and his abdomen with long, white streaks. His knees wobbled as Curt continued to batter him from behind for several more seconds, before his own orgasm released in a hefty groan of satisfaction.

A shudder rocked Curt's body as he leaned into Levi. "Wow."

"Yeah."

After a few minutes of catching their breaths, Curt removed his cock and slipped under the spray of the hot water. "Good thing you have a big hot water tank."

"Yep. If not, we would be showering in cold water by now."

Curt lathered soap all over his chest before he transferred some of the slick suds to Levi, washing his chest and groin in sensuous motions. Levi allowed the ministrations, enjoying Curt's hands on his flesh. His cock even stirred a little before giving him the hell no droop. After two orgasms so quick together, his cock was done for the night.

"I'm ready for bed. You wiped me out."

"Yeah, me too, although I don't know if I'll sleep much after napping earlier."

"You can rest. That's the big thing."

"I know. At least my headache didn't return. I'll be ready to help you do chores tomorrow."

"How did the books look?" Levi asked, stepping out after he rinsed off and drying himself with one of the fluffy white towels on the rack.

"Good. I think you're all set to run with it." Curt turned off the water and pulled a towel around his waist.

Droplets hung on his chest, making Levi want to catch them on his tongue. He shook his head. No used getting all wound up again. "About that?"

"About what?"

"What would you say to becoming a permanent member of my household?"

Curt held up his hands before he began to pace the bedroom. "Whoa, Levi. Let's not rush into anything." Agitation was clear in his movements as he raked his fingers through his wet hair.

"I'm not rushing, Curt."

He stopped and turned to face Levi. "Can you give me time to think about this?"

"Of course. How about you give me an answer by the end of finals? That's in three weeks. We have two more events before we have to be in Vegas and finals last four days, so you have almost a month to decide."

"Okay."

"I'm sorry. I didn't mean to freak you out."

"It's fine. I just didn't see it coming at all. I mean, we've been going along okay for the last couple of weeks, I didn't realize you were looking at a permanent arrangement."

Levi figured backpedaling was a good idea. Apparently, Curt wasn't ready for anything exclusive beyond what they had now. "If you aren't comfortable with something right now, that's okay. I'm thinking you could live here with me, do the finances for the ranch. We could be roommates, if nothing else. Maybe fuck buddies for a while. No pressure, you know?"

"Let's see how things go over the next few weeks. I'll give you my answer at the end of finals."

"Sounds good."

Levi grabbed a pair of boxers, slipped them on, and then climbed beneath the sheets on the bed. "Did you do the sheets today?"

"Yeah. I figured since I made them all dirty during my nap, it would be great to wash them and the comforter." Curt slid into the other side of the bed. "Besides, I love fresh washed sheets."

"Me too."

Silence enveloped them for several minutes after Levi turned out the light. Moonlight filtered through the curtains on the window, painting the room in a silvery white glow.

"Curt?"

"Yeah?"

"What are you looking for in this relationship?"

"I'm not sure I know what you mean."

"Are you looking for a few quick months of pleasure or do you want some kind of long term thing, because you know eventually, I want to find someone to spend the rest of my life with, build our dreams together kind of thing."

"You know, I really don't know. Eventually I want to find someone to spend eternity with, but I haven't really thought about it yet. My life is so up in the air with bull riding that I've never thought beyond that."

"What if you were to get seriously hurt and couldn't ride anymore?"

"I'll take it one day at a time, I guess."

"Hmm."

"You do realize you are pretty well set for life with your finances, the ranch, and your investments, right?"

Levi realized Curt changed the subject from a personal note with a quick twist to the question back to him. "I am?"

"Yeah. When I went through your investment portfolio earlier, I realized you've diversified nicely and have quite a little nest egg going there. Did you not realize you have several millions in investments that are paying you nice dividends?"

Levi sat straight up in the bed. "I do?"

Curt laughed as he put his hands behind his head. "Yes, you do. Good grief, man. I have to see who your investment broker is. He must just invest for you without you knowing about it. He's made you a very rich man."

"Wow." Levi leaned back on the bed. "I don't look at that stuff much."

"Obviously." Curt rolled over on his side and put his hand on his head to prop himself up. "You need to start paying more attention. It's no wonder that other guy took advantage of you."

"He was an asshole."

"I realize that, Levi, but you let him walk away with a lot of your money. You've managed to bounce back, but you should have had him arrested."

"I couldn't."

"Why?"

"Because I was the stupid one who gave him access to everything."

"Like you have me?"

Levi turned to face him. "I guess so. Maybe I should look more closely at what you've been doing."

"Now, you're going to stop trusting me?"

"Should I?"

Levi didn't like the way this conversation was headed, but he figured Curt was doing it to keep the pressure off himself so he didn't have to answer anything about his feelings. Oh well, he would be patient. Patience was a virtue and he had a lot of it these days. "We should get some sleep. Morning comes early on the ranch."

"Yes, it does. Good night, Levi."

"Good night, Curt."

Chapter Thirteen

Almost four damned weeks and not a word from Curt about whether they were going to make this a permanent thing or not. They'd continued to make love, almost living together in their room or on the ranch between events that were close enough they could go home. Curt did the books and kept them well organized. He even taught Levi how to do them so he wouldn't feel like Curt was taking over the financial part of things.

The whole time, Levi didn't have a clue what was going through his lover's mind and it was driving him batshit crazy.

He needed to concentrate. They'd both qualified for finals in the last weeks of the regular season, sitting twenty-eight and thirty-three in the standings. Points meant everything as the race for the title was neck-and-neck all the way to the bottom of the list. Each man was only separated by a few hundred points, which meant one ride could put you out or catapult you to the top of the standings. Each rider must do six rides over the four day event. Levi figured he had a shot at the World Championship title by a very thin margin, but he still had a chance. Curt did too, but a much smaller possibility of taking the title. They could both win the event title though which brought along a nice bonus of over two-hundred-thousand dollars. The big title came with a million dollar bonus. He really didn't need the money after what Curt told him, but he would love to have that coveted title of World

Champion before he retired. He hoped his shoulder held up. So far so good. It hadn't popped out of place again.

The first round was about to start. Everything was set. The bulls were either in the pens or in the chutes waiting for the riders. The crowd milled about getting beers, hotdogs, nachos or whatever before the event started.

The announcer began. "Welcome ladies and gentleman to the World Championship Bull Riding event of the year. This is the culmination of months of riding, prep work, praying, pain, and triumph, The World Championship. We have thirty-five of the best riders on the circuit who will be participating in six rides over four days, all ending with the crowning of this year's Champion Bull Rider for 2015 Help me welcome each rider as I call their name and they take their spot on top of the shark cage."

Each rider would be called by name from the last qualifier to the current leader, in that order until the final rider was announced.

Levi blew out a breath. This was it. The World Championship. He'd only been here twice before and never won the whole thing, never did well enough to win the event, but this year was his year. He could feel it in his bones. After this event, he would be able to walk away a winner if he so chose.

"How are you feeling? How's your shoulder?" Curt asked, coming to stand beside him as they waited for their name to be called.

"Good. It feels real good."

"Awesome." They watched as the lights went down. "Time to go meet the crowd."

Curt went out third in line with Levi bringing up a later spot since he'd taken a better rank in the standings.

After all the guys were announced, the crowd cheered as they took their places behind the chutes. Levi didn't have to ride for a bit, but Curt was one of the first three riders to go.

Curt climbed the back of the chute with his bull rope in hand, handed it off to the guy who would help him wrap it around the bull's chest, and then settled himself on the back of the bull. He waited for them to get it into place so he could secure it around his hand in preparation for his ride. Levi got up on the railing, holding onto Curt's vest in case they had to pull him free. The moment Curt had it rope wrapped correctly, he scooted into position and gave the nod.

The gate flew open.

The bull jumped straight up, whipped to the right, before spinning to the left. Curt held on with everything he had. The buzzer sounded just as he reached to release the rope. His eight second ride was perfection.

His score was eighty-nine point two.

Curt pumped his fists in the air after he climbed to his feet in the arena.

Levi met him at the exit shoot with a slap on the back and a fist bump. "Fantastic ride!"

"Thanks. It felt great. Smooth as butter." He frowned. "You're up pretty soon. Shouldn't you be stretching?"

"Yeah. I was headed to the back of the chutes as soon as I talked to you for a minute." Levi turned to head in the direction of one of the fences to stretch out his legs and arms.

Curt smacked him on the ass.

Levi's head turned to glance over his shoulder with what he knew had to be a stunned expression. Curt grinned and tipped his hat. Levi kept moving. *What the hell was that all about?*

He tied his bull rope around the chute fence, working in the rosin with his gloved hand to make the rope as sticky as he could. The concoction was his own ingredients, but it worked for him. A lot of the guys made their own.

Next, he stretched his muscles to warm them up before his ride. The only one he was really worried about was his shoulder. He couldn't afford to wrench it out of the socket again. It would kill his chances at the championship and it might even end his career.

It was his turn to get ready to ride. He looked behind him to find Curt at his side. "Go get 'em, tiger."

Levi blew out a breath as he climbed the fence to get into position. Several guys stood on the planks behind the chutes as he tossed his rope down for the men to wrap around the bull's chest. Straddling the huge animal was the easy part, getting ready was the easy part, staying on the two-thousand pound animal for eight seconds when he didn't want you there, that was the hard part.

With his thighs wrapped around the bull, he settled into position, wrapped his hand, and then gave the nod.

Everything happened in slow motion. The bull twisted right, before spinning back to the left. Both feet kicked out behind him. He jumped straight up, landing with a bone-jarring, teeth-snapping thud.

The buzzer sounded.

Levi released his hand, jumping free at the first moment he could.

He rolled in the dirt before jumping to his feet and heading for the exit.

The bull charged him, making him run for the safety of the fence. He managed to escape to the exit just before the bull banged his horns against the railing. *That was too close.*

"Are you okay?" Curt asked, rushing to his side.

"Yeah, he missed me by a few inches."

"You had your back to him when he charged. I thought for sure he'd have you at the fence."

"Nope. I managed to run fast enough. You know what they say. You don't have to outrun the bull, just the other guy running with you. The bull fighters got him."

"Scared the shit out of me. Don't do that again."

"What? Ride bulls? Not happenin', skipper." Disappointment rushed through him as he looked up at the score board. His ride didn't garner the points he was hoping for at eighty-six even. "Shit. My score sucked."

"You'll pick it up in the next round."

"I hope so, otherwise, I need a couple of guys to get bucked off."

The first day, they would ride twice. The second day once, the third day twice, and the fourth day once for the final title round. These four days were nerve wracking to say the least, but after they'd ridden for the second time today, they could grab some grub, get a beer and relax until tomorrow.

They continued to watch as each rider went through their turn. Several got bucked off, while a few more rode through their eight seconds. At the end of round one, Levi had gained two spots in the stands, while Curt gained five.

By the end of the second round, Levi had gained two more spots in the standings while Curt gained one.

Levi was beat. His shoulder hurt, hell, his whole body hurt from being whipped around and thrown to the ground. *Man, I feel like I'm really out of shape.*

"You okay?"

"Yeah, just sore tonight." Levi rotated his arm to relieve some of the stiffness.

"Let's grab some food, a couple of beers, and then some shut-eye so we can be ready for tomorrow. I can help you stretch it out in the room." Curt waggled his eyebrows.

"At least we only have to ride once in the next round."

"True. Tomorrow will be easier than tonight."

As they moved toward the locker room to grab their gear, Colt Tucker stepped in front of their path, blocking them from moving any farther.

"Problem, Colt?"

"I know all about you, Levi."

"You know what?"

"You're a fucking queer." Colt moved closer so he was almost nose-to-nose with Levi.

The other man stood about the same height, but he wasn't near as bulky as Levi. He was thin and wiry.

"I like to think of myself as gay, but you label it anyway you like."

Colt glanced at Curt and then back to him. "You two are fuck buddies, getting your rocks off by fucking each other in the ass. You need to get the hell out of here. Leave the circuit. We don't want your kind here."

"What I do in my own bedroom is none of your business. I'm not coming onto you. I don't even like you, so you don't have to worry about me fucking you in any shape or form. My sexual preference has nothing to do with how I ride bulls and I don't flaunt it in front of others on the circuit, so you can kiss my ass, Colt. Find someone else to intimidate because I'm not afraid of you. I'll kick your ass into next week given half a chance. Back off, asshole."

He stared at Colt for several long seconds before the other cowboy backed down and let them pass.

"You should have punched him," Curt said as they reached the locker room.

"Nah. He's not worth the bruised knuckles."

"He called you a queer, a fucking queer at that."

"It doesn't matter. His opinion is his own. He doesn't like anybody if my sources are right. He's a loner, keeps to himself most of the time, and doesn't have very many friends." Levi dropped his voice to a whisper as he leaned in a little closer. "He's probably jealous because I'm fucking you."

"No way."

"Yes, way."

Curt grinned.

What does that mean? Is he happy we're fucking? Does he think about what it would be like to be in a permanent relationship with me? Levi shook his head as he bent down to grab his gear bag. *I need to quit thinking about this shit. I'm driving myself nuts, but he only has a few more days to tell me yes or no.*

Once Curt had his zipped bag in hand, they headed back out the door, down the hall, and out toward the parking lot. A huge crowd of fans hung out near the entrance waiting for autographs. They spent the next thirty minutes signing things, taking pictures, and schmoozing with the crowd. This was the part of the evening Levi enjoyed the most. The fans were everything to him. Several other riders worked the crowd as well. This was their time to get some one-on-one connection with their favorite rider and the guys obliged.

He and Curt worked their way toward his truck. After the last trip out to his place, they'd left Curt's truck at his house and just took Levi's. There wasn't any reason for them to drive separate vehicles now with them practically living together. "The honkytonk?"

"Yeah. I need a couple of beers to chill the hell out. This adrenaline high is giving me a headache."

"Are you okay?"

"Yeah, but I think I'll take some Tylenol or something before it gets too bad."

They made their way to the bar and moseyed on inside to find the place packed with people. The bar had a couple of spots open, so they took two bar stools, signaled for the bartender to bring them a beer each, and got comfortable.

The crowd was huge. A sea of cowboy hats, rhinestones, and Wranglers jeans told the tale of how popular this particular bar was, especially after an event apparently. Several of the other bull riders made their way inside as Levi sipped his beer and watched the people moving through. He waved to a few of the guys as they walked by, trying to find a spot. Some people stood, others danced, and a small amount managed to secure tables to sit at.

Curt leaned toward Levi, bumping his chest into Levi's shoulder. "Two girls have us in their sights."

"Oh yeah?"

"Yeah." He got close enough to Levi's ear, he could feel the heat of Curt's breath on his flesh. Shivers raced down his spine. "You into women at all?"

"Not really. They don't do much for me." *So this is it. Curt won't be able to give up pussy for me, ever, it seems.*

"Pussy is nice every once in a while."

"I'm gay, Curt. Take it or leave it."

"What are you saying, Levi?"

"I don't want pussy. I want you." He tipped the beer to his lips, draining the liquid in a few gulps. "You haven't given me an answer to my question."

"I still have a couple of days."

"Obviously, you've already made up your mind if you're pussy scoping."

"I'm not."

"You brought it up."

Curt set his beer on the bar. "I'm done. Let's get out of here."

"Fine."

They headed for the door, weaving their way through the throng of people, trying to keep out of everyone's way. Curt bumped into someone, spilling beer down the front of a lady's dress.

"You fucker!" The guy swung, hitting Curt in the left eye, dropping him back into the crowd as they parted like the red sea.

He hit the ground and was out cold.

"What the fuck!" Levi dropped to his knees next to Curt. He didn't move, didn't moan, nothing. "Curt?" Curt's body began to jerk in weird lurching motions that were uncoordinated and scary. "Someone call an ambulance." Levi turned his lover onto his side as he began to vomit. The crowd retreated, giving them a little room.

Within several minutes, the ambulance arrived. As the paramedics began to treat him, Levi kneeled near Curt's head, touching the curls at the top of his head as he whispered soothing words. He didn't care what others thought. This was the man he loved lying in a pool of vomit as medical personnel worked on him. Levi answered as many questions as he could about Curt, including his age, address, medical history, and so on, but it didn't seem enough. Nothing would be enough to make Curt better.

As they put him on the gurney, Levi walked out behind them. "I'm coming with you."

"Sorry, you can't ride with us, but you can follow us if you like."

"Fine."

Levi ran for his truck as they put Curt into the ambulance, turned on the lights, and sped away. He caught them just as they turned the first corner. He didn't care if he was running lights. He didn't care if the police chased him across the city, he was going to be there for Curt.

The last few minutes rolled through his mind as he tried to make sense of what happened. The guy really hadn't hit Curt that hard to cause him to lose consciousness, he didn't think, and what was that jerking stuff going on? He'd never seen that before even for as long as he'd ridden in the circuit. He wished he could talk to Doc and find out what it might be, but they didn't have time. Hopefully the emergency room would be able to tell him something quickly.

The ambulance pulled into the hospital emergency room bay while he found a close parking spot. He rushed up to the back as they were taking Curt out on the gurney.

"You won't be able to go in this way. Go through the double doors to the left there, tell the receptionist who you are with, and the doctor will come out to talk to you as soon as he knows anything."

"But, I'm with him."

"I know. I'm sorry, but you can't go in there while they are working on him."

Levi sighed, closing his eyes as he squeezed the bridge of his nose between his finger and thumb. It would be a long night at this rate.

After what seemed like hours, a doctor came out of the double doors and asked if anyone was there for Curt Walsh. Levi stood and came forward. "I am. I'm a friend."

"Come with me."

Levi followed the doctor back through the doors and down a long hallway. Several curtained off areas stood to each side. He could see people lying on gurneys similar to what Curt had been on as they passed. The doctor didn't say anything while they moved down the hall.

When they finally reached the last curtain to the right, the doctor waved Levi in between the two panels.

The doctor moved to Curt's bedside before turning to face Levi. "What can you tell me about his recent history? Anything to do with his head or brain."

Levi looked at Curt lying on the wide sheet. His face was pale and drawn. He didn't look like the man Levi had come to love with all his heart. "He had a concussion about two months ago after a nasty spill on a bull."

"He's a bull rider?"

"Yes."

"Has he had concussions before?"

Levi shrugged as he continued to watch the slow, steady beeping of the monitor over Curt's head. As long as it continued to beep, he figured everything would be fine. *Just keep beeping.* "I'm not sure."

"Was he out for some time with this episode he had not too long ago?"

"Yes. He was unconscious for several minutes and confused for some time after that."

"Hmm."

"What's wrong with him, Doc?" Levi asked, touching Curt's hand before pulling it back. The flesh was warm and strong, all good things. Curt would get better. He had to.

"He's suffered a brain hemorrhage."

"What is that?"

"A bleed on the brain. I understand someone hit him at the bar?"

"Yes. Knocked him out cold."

"I believe that's what caused this although from what you've told me, he probably had a weak spot on his brain from the riding accident. The blow at the bar just managed to cause a rupture."

"What's this all mean?"

The doctor waved his hand to indicate Curt lying on the stark white sheets. "Well, as you can see, he is still unconscious and that isn't good. We've done a CAT scan and it shows a large bleed on the right side of his brain. We will have to admit him to monitor the pressure on his skull and brain tissue throughout the night. We may have to do surgery if we can't control the swelling with medications."

"Oh God." Levi sank into a chair sitting near the bedside. *This isn't good.*

"I'm sorry. Are you friends?"

"Yes."

"I have to tell you, there may be some deficit when this is all said and done. He's basically suffered a stroke which could cause many problems including weakness in extremities, inability to walk, he might not be able to talk, and a host of other things. We won't know the extent of the problems until he wakes up and we can evaluate him in these areas. He also had a seizure from what the paramedics said."

"Yeah, at the bar."

"He hasn't had any since, so that's a good thing."

Levi rubbed his forehead with his fingers. *What the hell am I going to do?*

"There are plenty of good things about his condition too, no seizures, he's breathing on his own, he's moved his fingers a few times, and his pupils are equal and reactive. These are good signs. He could make a complete recovery without any problems. We have to stay hopeful."

"Thanks, Doc."

"He'll be admitted shortly to ICU. You won't be able to stay with him in the room and you can only visit for five minutes at a time, once an hour."

"I appreciate everything you've done. Can I stay with him until they move him?"

"Yes. You can check with the nurses when they get him upstairs, give them your number and tell them to contact you should his condition change." The doctor rubbed his tired looking eyes. "Do you know his family? Can you contact them?"

"I'm sure he has their numbers in his cell phone, which would have been in his pocket of his clothes."

"Clothing is in the bag on the counter there."

"Thanks. I'll get it and try to contact them."

"We appreciate it."

"No problem." Levi stood and moved toward the bag on the counter to retrieve Curt's phone. He didn't know Curt's parents, but this was for Curt. He figured they would want to know about their son's accident.

Once he retrieved the phone, he stepped out of Curt's room and down the hall to make the call. He found a number in the contacts under parents, so he stepped into a vacant room, and hit talk.

A woman picked up on the second ring. "Curt?"

"Hi. No, this is Levi Bond. I'm a friend of Curt's. The one he's been traveling with on the circuit lately?"

"Ah. Yes, he's talked about you the few times he's called home. What's he done now?"

"Done?"

"He's always getting into scrapes. You know, fights and whatnot. Is he in jail or something?"

"No, ma'am. He's not in jail."

"Then why are you calling from his phone?"

"There's been an accident. You know about him having a concussion several weeks ago?"

"He mentioned it, yes, but I thought everything was okay."

"It was until he got hit at a bar tonight for spilling beer on some woman accidently. It knocked him out cold. I'm at the hospital with him and they say he's had a stroke. He's still unconscious so they don't know the extent of the injury, but his brain is swelling and they are trying to get that to come down."

"Oh my."

"I don't have much else to tell you until he's awake. I can call you as soon as that happens."

"Yes, please. His father and I would appreciate it very much, Levi. Thank you."

"You're welcome, ma'am." His shoulders dropped in relief since he wasn't sure how Curt's parents would react to him calling. He didn't know how much they knew about his and Curt's relationship and he didn't want to rock the boat. "I'll call you as soon as I know something."

"Thank you."

"You're welcome." He hung up the phone before heading back down the hall. He'd seen a nurse walk into Curt's room a few moments ago and he hoped they would be moving him soon. He'd have to head back to the hotel for the night to get some shut-eye if he could, but he would be back first thing in the morning.

Shit. We were supposed to ride at four tomorrow afternoon. "Curt is obviously out for the duration. He won't be able to ride in the rest of the finals. I have to though. I can't not ride."

When he reached Curt's beside, the nurse was unhooking things and transferring them to the bed. "Oh, hi. I'll be moving him upstairs here in a second. You're welcome to walk up with me."

"Thanks."

Several moments later, they had him situated in the bed in the ICU. The nurses explained the visitation policy, before shooing Levi out of the room. "I'll be back tomorrow to see him since I can't stay up here. Here is my number. Call me if anything changes. I'll have it by the bed."

"Certainly, sir."

"I appreciate it."

"No problem. Rest easy. He's in good hands."

Rest didn't come that night at all. Levi tossed and turned thinking about all the things that could happen to Curt, how he could be affected by this, and what their lives would be like should he be wheelchair bound, unable to move, or unable to speak. He would stand beside his lover no matter what, but they hadn't come to any real solution to whether Curt wanted him. Now he may never know.

Chapter Fourteen

The next morning bright and early found Levi at the hospital. He'd showered and shaved quickly before grabbing his keys and heading over to be at Curt's bedside, hoping he would be awake, alert, talking, and moving everything just fine. It wasn't to be. Curt still hadn't awoken.

"He's better this morning," the nurse said, as Levi moved to Curt's side.

"How? He's not awake."

"No, but the pressure on his brain is better. He'll hopefully become conscious today and we can assess his function level." She glanced at Levi. "Are you two really bull riders?"

Levi fingered the sheet next to Curt's hand, wanting to touch him, but holding back. "Yeah."

"That is so cool. I love to watch you guys ride. What's your name?"

"Levi Bond."

The woman grinned so big, Levi thought her face would split wide open. "I know you! You are one of my favorites."

"Thanks."

"Are you two good friends?"

"Yeah, something like that." He touched Curt's fingers, running the pad of his index finger over the back of Curt's hand.

"Oh, I get it. You're like together, right?"

He was tired of denying things. He wanted people to know he loved this man and he wasn't afraid to show his feelings anymore. "Yeah, we are."

"That's cool." She bounced on her toes in excitement. "I'm so thrilled to meet you. I wish I had something to have you autograph."

"Can we talk about this later? Isn't there something you need to be doing for him?"

She waved her hand in dismissal. "No. We've already done everything for him this morning we can do. It's a waiting game now."

"Oh."

"You won't be able to stay much longer. The rule is five minutes per hour, so you'll have to go soon."

He continued to caress Curt's hand, thrilled when Curt moved a finger in response. "He moved his fingers!"

"Yes. He's been doing that most of the night, and moving his feet too, which is a good sign, although we won't know the extent of any weakness for a bit."

"Thank you, God."

"Things are looking pretty good. If he'd regain consciousness, it would be even better, but as I said, we expect him to by this afternoon." She glanced at the clock on the wall. "I'm sorry, but you'll have to leave now. You can come back in an hour."

"I will. I have to let the riders association know what happened and that he won't be riding for the rest of the finals."

"Oh, that's right! The finals are in town. How cool is that?"

"I will be back."

"Right. Good. See you then!"

Levi walked out of the double doors keeping the ICU separate from the rest of the hospital, and down the hall toward the elevator. He had some things to do today and time was wasting.

That afternoon, Levi found himself getting ready to ride. He had one round to do this afternoon in the finals and, by damn, he planned to make this count for Curt.

It sucked not having his spot man at his shoulder when his turn came up, but he planned to ride for the full eight seconds, get a fantastic score and move up in the standings. Winning the world championship had become his goal at the beginning of this year, now it was his soul focus. He would do anything for the title, the buckle, and the picture on the wall.

After his ride, he pumped his fists in the air. It felt good, looked good, and he just knew he'd scored well. The numbers flashed on the screen. Ninety-two points. "Yes!" He pressed his fingers to his lips, blowing a kiss to the crowd as they cheered with a roar. That score put him in first place for the round and fifth overall in the standings. He had three more rides to go before he could count his chickens, but he had a shot at the World Championship title if he continued to ride this well.

He headed for the locker room to check his phone. He'd been hoping for an update from the nurse at the hospital all afternoon since he hadn't been able to get back to check on Curt since this morning. Circuit functions had kept him busy and everyone wanted to know what was up with his riding partner. When he reached into his bag, he noticed the phone blinking. He pulled up the messages and listened. Curt was awake, although there were no further updates.

Unfortunately, now that he was in first place, he couldn't leave the event until everyone had ridden. Besides, he wanted to watch to see how his standings were at the end of the night. The best riders on the circuit were up after him and they were higher in the standings, which meant if they rode their bulls to the end, he would probably stay in fifth. He was okay with that for tonight.

By the time everyone had ridden, he was now in fourth place. One of the final riders for the evening got bucked off his bull, dropping him into fifth and moving Levi up one notch.

The best thing was he'd won the round with his score of ninety-two. When he went out to accept the congratulations of the circuit and the fans, he had to tell them, this round was for Curt.

The minute he could get away, he rushed back to the hospital. When he walked into Curt's room, he was sitting up in bed watching television.

"How are you feeling?"

"Like, um, I was, um, hit by a, um, bus."

"I don't think that guy was that big, but yeah, you took a good shot. Did the doctors come in to talk to you?"

Curt shrugged.

"Are you having trouble with words?"

Curt nodded. "I can't—what's the word—um. Remember."

"I know. It's okay."

"No!"

"Yes, it'll be fine."

"No!"

"Don't get your blood pressure up. I know you're having a hard time forming words and getting out what you want to say, but you are doing a hundred percent better than you were yesterday." Levi took the chair beside the bed.

"I saw."

"What? The riding today?"

"Yes. You won."

"Yeah. Mine was ninety-two points."

"Cool!" Curt lifted his hand to fist bump Levi, but he couldn't hold it up very well.

"I'm now fourth in the standings."

Curt smiled. The left half of his face drooped some.

Wow. This is worse than I thought. "From what I understand, you've had a stroke from a ruptured vessel in your head. They think there might have been a weak one after the shot you took a couple of months back, and the guy hitting you at the bar made it rupture. They said you might have some problems with speech, remembering, walking, and stuff like that for a while, but now that you are awake they can see exactly what's up and work with you."

"Levi?" A frown drew down the inside edges of his eyebrows as he refused to meet Levi's gaze. His hands were fisted in the bed sheets like he was afraid of something.

"Yeah?"

"Don't leave me."

He grabbed Curt's hand, smoothing out the fist until it relaxed in his grasp. "Leave you? I'm not leaving you."

"I'm afraid."

"I know."

"I, um. Can't ride."

"No, you won't be able to ride for a while, but we'll work on that. We have bulls at the house you can get on and everything. You'll get back in the arena, just not this year."

"I'm sorry."

"There isn't anything to be sorry about."

"I." Curt pulled Levi's hand up to his mouth. "Love you."

"What did you say?"

"I love you."

"You do?"

Curt nodded. "I'm afraid for us."

"Don't be. We'll be fine because I love you too. I want to spend the rest of my life with you."

"Sure?"

"Yes. After the finals, we'll go home, back to my place. You can recuperate and get better. We'll have a few months off before next year starts and we'll go from there. You'll be back in the arena in no time."

"Win this year."

"I'm going to do my best, buddy. For you."

"No, for you."

Later that evening, they moved Curt to a regular room out in the hospital where Levi could stay as long as he wanted. They spent hours watching television, holding hands, being together, and talking as best they could with Curt's limited ability. Levi knew they would be okay, everything would be okay now that he knew Curt loved him.

"I need to call your parents."

"No!"

Curt grasped Levi's hand in a hard hold. His grip seemed a lot stronger than it was earlier. "I talked to your mom the other day when you were unconscious. I need to give them an update."

"No, don't call them."

"I have to, Curt. They want to know."

"They don't care about me."

"Yes, they do, they're your parents."

"They don't."

"It'll be fine."

Curt seemed to want to say more, but held back. Levi wasn't sure what the issue was with Curt's parents, but he obviously felt they were standoffish or something. Levi didn't know the whole story, but someday he would get Curt to tell him.

"Okay."

Levi pulled out Curt's phone and dialed. His mother answered after a couple of rings.

"Hi, Mrs. Walsh, this is Levi Bond again."

"Hi, Levi. How is Curt?"

"He's awake and doing much better, although there are some problems."

"What kind of problems?"

"His speech is delayed. He is having trouble finding words. I think his arm is a little weak, but I won't know until the doctor's do an assessment on him to see what else."

"Oh my."

"They'll be releasing him in a few days and I plan to take him home with me."

"Why? I don't understand. He should come home to us so we can see to his needs."

"He wants to be with me at my place." Levi switched the phone to his other ear as he got up and began to pace the room. He could feel Curt's gaze on his back while he moved from the window to the bed. "Listen, the doctor just walked in. I'll call you back as soon as I know something. Talk to you soon." He hung up the phone quickly, unsure of what Curt wanted him to say to his mother. Did he want him to tell her they were in a relationship? He didn't think it was his place to do that, but how would they explain his wanting to be at Levi's place rather than going home?

"Why did, um, you lie?"

"I didn't know how much they knew about us."

"Nothing."

"You haven't told them?"

"No. They wouldn't, um, understand."

"They don't know you are bi-sexual?"

"No."

Levi took a seat in the chair again, leaning forward to rest his elbows on his knees as he contemplated his lover. "You can't keep it a secret from them if we are planning a future together."

"I know."

"Then what do you want me to tell them is the reason you are staying with me instead of coming home?

Curt shrugged just as the doctor came into the room.

"How are you feeling this evening, Mr. Walsh?"

"Good."

Levi frowned in Curt's direction. Obviously Curt wasn't going to tell the doctor what he needed to know about his condition. *Well to hell with that. I'll tell him.* "He's been having trouble finding the right words when he wants to speak, and I think he has a little weakness in his arm."

"Let me take a look." After several tests including strength, walking, repeating phrases the doctor said, and ability to problem solve, the doctor gave them the news. "You're having trouble speaking, you do have a little weakness to your right arm and hand, but your ability to walk has been maintained. We will have a swallow evaluation done on you to make sure you aren't having any problems with that, but overall, you will probably be able to do rehabilitation and regain the strength in your hand and arm. As for the speech patterns, we'll have to see, but you can work on that with a speech therapist too, after you're released."

"When will that be?"

"Probably day after tomorrow since he's alert, awake, and can function to some degree. I will have physical therapy work with you tomorrow and the next day to teach you some exercises to do for your extremities to strengthen them until you can get home physical therapy started. Where will you be going?"

"To my place in Mystique, Oklahoma."

"Okay. We will see what we can find to set that up before you all leave for home. Make sure to let the nurse know so she can give it to the case manager. They'll get it ready for you before you leave Las Vegas."

"Will he be able to travel by car all right?"

"Should be, but don't push for long days of driving. Stop, rest, stretch, and relax."

"What about sex?" Curt asked, his words clear as day. Levi smiled as he looked down at his hands where they rested on his thighs.

"Sex?" the doctor asked, as he looked back and forth between the two of them.

"Can I have sex?"

"Of course, if you're careful. Everything should work fine since you don't seem to have any deficits in your lower extremities, just your right hand and arm. No riding bulls for a while though. Get your strength back before you try doing that."

"All right. Thanks, Doctor."

"You're welcome. I will see you tomorrow to check on you. Have the nurse call me if you need anything specific. Until then, rest. No running around the room, but you should get up and walk the halls. You need to make sure you don't lose function in your legs by being in the bed the whole time you're here."

"I will walk."

"Good and keep talking. It will help you form the words better and help the synapses in your brain to function beyond the damage that has occurred."

"All right. I will."

The doctor shook Curt's hand and then Levi's before he made his way to the door. "I want you out in the halls at least three times a day while you're still here. So get up before you are ready for bed and walk."

"Yes, sir."

The doctor smiled. "See you tomorrow."

As the door slowly shut behind him, Levi turned to Curt, took his hand in the palm of his own and squeezed. "Now, what are we going to tell your parents?"

"I don't know."

"We can tell them the truth."

"Not, um, a good, um, idea."

"What do you suggest then?"

Curt frowned as he picked the blanket beneath his fingers. Levi couldn't tell what was going through his mind, but he knew he struggled with the rights words. "Don't tell them anything."

"I have to tell them something, Curt. What reason do you have for going to my house rather than home? If they don't know we are together, then it's kind of odd since we've really only been roommates on the road for a few months."

"Tell her…" His face wrinkled in concentration.

Levi let him pick his words carefully. This could mean their future or the end of their relationship if he didn't stand up for them as a couple.

"Tell her about us."

"Are you sure you don't want to do that?" Levi asked even though relief washed through him.

"No. I can't. My words won't come right."

"Do we want to do that in person maybe? I think that would be the better choice than on the phone, don't you?"

"Maybe."

"We'll plan on going there before we go home then. After finals."

"Will you stay tonight here with me?"

"I'd better not even though I would love to. Those chairs aren't comfortable and I'm afraid it would kill my shoulder to be crunched in it before I ride tomorrow. I have two rides to do in the next round so I need to be on my game if I'm going to win."

"I know."

"Let me call her back and tell her we'll be there before the middle of next week. We have to take the travel slow. I would imagine no more than six hours in the car at a time would be a good point to start with. We can adjust more or less as you tolerate it one way or the other." Levi picked up the phone, found Curt's parents number, and hit talk.

"Curt?"

"No, it's Levi. Curt is having a really hard time finding the words to speak so he asked me to call you back."

"That's okay, Levi. I'm glad you called."

"I wanted to let you know he's doing better. The doctor said he has some speech problems they will work on and a little weakness to his right hand and arm, but he can walk okay, which is good. He will have some physical therapy while he's here, be discharged in a couple of days, and as soon as finals are over, we'll be heading your way. He wants to visit you and his father."

"Wonderful! I can't wait to see him and again, thank you so much for being there for him. I know you two haven't been friends very long, but you've been great for him. I'm so glad you two hooked up."

Levi smiled to himself at the inside joke of what hooked up meant to him and what it meant to her. "Me too, Mrs. Walsh. Listen, I can't talk long. I have to get back to the hotel and rest up for tomorrow's round, but Curt's thinking about you and I'm sure he'll be glad to see you when we get there next week." Curt made a face at him. "We will have to take the drive slow. The doctor suggested that so he could get out and stretch while we travel."

"Good. We'll see you next week some time then."

"Yes, ma'am."

"Thank you again."

"Talk to you later."

"Goodbye."

"Bye for now." He hung up the phone and put it back on the bedside table. "Are you going to tell me why you have a problem with your parents?"

"They don't support me. Never have."

"In what ways?"

In broken sentences, Curt told Levi about growing up in a household where his parents didn't seem to care if he was around or not. They never supported him doing rodeo rides in high school. He worked shoveling shit at a neighbor's farm to pay for a horse and saddle so he could do roping events besides bull riding even though they had plenty of money to help him if they wanted to. His father never seemed to want to teach him anything about ranching, just shoving him away when he tried to help. His mother was too wrapped up in working her way up the corporate ladder to care about her son. They doted on his sister and look how she turned out, drug addicted, on welfare, didn't know who the father of her kids were, and a leech in every sense of the word. "They didn't want a son."

"I don't believe that."

"They don't come to events."

"So. Mine haven't been to that many either. They have the ranch to run. They can't always leave."

"Once, Levi, just once I would like for them to come."

"Have you told them that?"

"No."

"Why not?"

"I don't know."

"Maybe if they knew how much it meant to you, they would have made more of an effort to come to one that was close. We usually do an event in Amarillo once a year." He took Curt's hand in his. "Maybe if you asked them to, they would."

"I have. They're too busy."

"As young adults raising a family, most of the time parents are too busy feeding the children. It sounds like they wanted you to be self-sufficient growing up and then did a complete one-eighty with your sister. They might have been trying to figure out the best way to raise their children. You should give them a little bit of a break."

"I haven't heard my parents say they love me in years."

"I'm not trying to make excuses for them, Curt. I'm just trying to say there might have been extenuating circumstances or they might be lousy parents, but a little effort on your part could go a long way."

"Fine. I'll try when we go."

"Good." Levi stood, tugging at the thighs of his jeans to pull them back down into place over his boots. "Rest and I'll see you tomorrow after I ride."

"I love you."

"I love you too." He leaned in, kissing Curt full on the mouth with more hunger than he thought possible. He wanted his lover more than anything, but he knew they would have to play things by ear. Curt had a long road to recovery, but Levi planned to be there every step of the way.

Chapter Fifteen

"It all comes down to this, folks. One ride. If Levi Bond rides this bull for his eight second ride, he'll win the championship."

The entire crowd was silent. Twenty thousand people didn't make a sound.

Levi could hear himself breathe.

His stomach knotted.

The bull banged his horns against the side of the chute. The clang echoed in the silence.

One ride. How in the fuck had it come down to one ride for all of it? He didn't know, but here he sat on the back of his final bull, Lucifer's Chaos, waiting to ride as he wrapped his hand for the final time of the season. This was it. Stay on and win, buck off and go home in second place.

This bull was rank. Top of the line. His buck off rate was phenomenal. He'd only been ridden twice in his entire career as a bucking bull.

Levi had to ride like his life depended on it.

Curt watched from his seat behind the chutes.

Levi looked up and caught his gaze. Curt smiled and gave him a thumbs-up. He could do this.

He nodded.

The gate flew open as the bull turned to his left, shot out of the chute, and jumped straight up. His body twisted to the left while his hind end went right.

Levi's right shoulder burned as it took the brunt of the movement. His left arm whipped back and forth. His thighs ached as he gripped the bull with his legs, spurring the beast with his boots to make it look like an even better ride.

He counted in his head. *One Mississippi, two Mississippi, three Mississippi.*

His body slid sideways.

He corrected by pulling himself back up on the back of the bull.

Four Mississippi, five Mississippi, six Mississippi.

The buzzer sounded, indicating the end of his eight second ride.

He pulled on the end of his bull rope to release his hand so he could jump free.

He'd done it!

World Champion!

The crowd went wild, screaming and chanting his name as he pumped his fists in the air in triumph. He ran around the entire length of the arena in a wild sprint as the announcer said his name and talked about what an amazing comeback from twenty-eighth in the standings to win the entire thing.

"What an astonishing feat! Levi Bond has won it all! World Champion!"

The circuit reporter stopped him as he made his way to where they would present him with the buckle, the trophy and the check for over one-million dollars.

"How does it feel to win it all, Levi?"

"Fantastic! Oh my God. I can't believe it."

"This has been an astounding year for you after your shoulder injury of a couple of months ago. Did you do anything different to train for such a fantastic string of qualifying rides?"

"Nothing different except fall in love."

"Well, that's great, Levi. I wish you all the happiness in the world. Go accept your earnings."

The announcer pulled him up on top of the shark cage. "Ladies and gentlemen. I give you your 2015 World Champion Bull Rider, Levi Bond."

* * * *

Three days later, they pulled into the yard of Curt's parent's ranch. He knew his lover was nervous, scared, and sweating over telling his folks about their relationship, but it had to be done. They couldn't move on with their lives without at least telling them about it. They didn't really need their blessing, although that would make the whole thing much sweeter.

"You okay?"

Curt smoothed the thighs of his jeans with his hands. Levi figured he was wiping the sweat from his palms.

"Yeah, let's get this over with."

They watched through the windshield of Levi's truck as Curt's mom stepped out of the house. She reminded Levi of a '50s housewife with her hair back in a bun, an apron around her waist and a sweater around her shoulders.

"Curtis!"

"Curtis?"

"That's my full name."

"I guess I should have guessed that."

"I should have told you."

"No biggie, Curtis."

Curt smiled and shook his head before they stepped out of the truck on either side. His mother rushed down the two small stairs on the porch, and grabbed Curt in a hug.

"I'm so glad you're home."

"You are?"

"Yes. You haven't been home in months, it seems." She stepped back, wiping tears from her cheeks. "You look pretty good. How do you feel?"

"Weak sometimes, but pretty good today."

"Let's get you in the house and sitting on the couch. I can bring you something to drink and eat while we wait for your father to come in from the barn. I'm sure he heard you pull in. If not, I'll go get him in a bit."

"I'm okay to walk, Mom. In fact I need to so I keep the strength and coordination in my legs."

"Well, go slowly then. I don't want you tripping or anything."

They walked into the house, through the entryway, into the living room. The décor spoke of hominess, long time antiques, and special memories. Levi liked the feel. He also liked Curt's mother. Long drapes hung on the windows, but were pulled back to let the sunshine in. Leather furniture graced the room in a pattern meant to bring people together with the center focus being the huge fireplace along the wall. Wrought iron tables brought the whole thing together.

"What a great room," Levi said, taking a seat next to Curt on the couch.

"Thank you. This is one of my favorite rooms in the house. I love to sit in here with a book, a fire, and a cup of tea."

"I certainly can picture you in the chair over there, with your feet on the ottoman, relaxing with a good book."

She wiped her hands absently on the apron around her waist. "What can I get you boys to drink?"

"A soda would be good, Mom."

"Okay. Levi?"

"Soda is fine for me as well."

"Coming right up." She disappeared through the doorway at the back of the room for a couple of moments before returning with two cans and a couple of glasses with some ice. "Here you go."

"Thanks."

"How long are you boys planning to stay? Do I need to get your room ready, Curtis?"

"No, we aren't staying the night. We need to get to Levi's so I can start therapy in the morning."

Her face reflected her disappointment as a frown drew her lips down. "Oh. I see. I wish you could stay a couple of days, honey. We haven't seen you in months."

"I know."

The back porch screen banged as his father came in from the barn. "Where is everyone?"

"In the front room, dear."

His father came through the kitchen doorway, bigger than life. Standing at what Levi guessed to be six-foot-five with huge, broad shoulders, the man filled out the doorway. His hair had gone completely white and his face was leathered with lines from so much time in the sun.

"Curtis."

"Dad."

"How are you feeling?"

"Good. A little weak, but good overall."

"I'm glad. It's nice to see you." He moved to the end of the couch. "You must be Levi."

"Yes, sir."

"It's nice to meet you. Thank you for being there for our boy. You've been a good friend."

"I should get dinner started." His mother got to her feet, kissed her husband on the lips, and then moved through the room toward the kitchen.

His father took the chair she'd vacated. "You won the championship, eh Levi?"

"Yes, sir."

"What a fantastic run you had there toward the end. What was it? Eight bulls in a row with a qualifying ride?"

"Yes, sir."

"Where are you from, son?"

"Mystique, Oklahoma, outside Stillwater."

"Ah, yes. I've been there a time or two buying stock."

"How's the ranch doing, Dad?"

"Fine, fine." He waved his hand to dismiss Curt as if he hadn't even talked. "What do you do for a living, Levi?"

"I have a ranch that I raise cattle, horses, and a few bucking bulls we are hoping to get contracted for the circuit next year."

"Interesting. How are things on your place? I know beef prices are down right now."

Curt's face looked forlorn. He'd been basically dismissed by his father. Levi could now see what Curt had been talking about all along with thinking his parents didn't care. It appeared they didn't, but Levi wasn't giving up. Nope, not yet. They still had to break the news of their relationship to his parents, and it might be a breaking point in the tumultuous relationship he already had with them.

"Things are well, sir. Curt has taken over doing my finances and tells me the ranch is very well-off financially. I owe everything to him. If he hadn't straightened me out, who knows where I would have been and with winning the championship, that million dollar check will come in handy."

"Good. Curtis was always a wiz with numbers. He got straight As in school."

"I didn't think you noticed, Dad."

"Of course, I noticed. I kept pretty good tabs on you."

Emotion tainted Curt's words as he rattled off complete sentences, blasting his father with everything he'd been bottling up inside for years. "You didn't give a shit enough to keep tabs on me. You never cared enough to worry about what I was doing before, during, or after school. You never came to events. You didn't let me help with anything. You haven't been to one of my bull riding events since I started on the circuit. You don't care about me at all." Curt climbed to his feet. "Let's get out of here, Levi. These people care nothing for me."

"Hold on one second, son. Your mother and I love you."

"News to me. That's the first time I've heard you say it in years."

Curt's dad stood so he and Curt were almost toe-to-toe. "I'm sorry you feel we didn't care about you. This ranch takes man power to run. The reason I didn't let you get involved so much in the ranch was because I didn't want you wasting your teenage years working on this place. You worked for the neighbor for your riding gear. It taught you to work for your money, rather than your mother and I handing it to you. You never really showed an inclination to want to learn about the ranch and how it was run."

"I wanted to learn. You wouldn't teach me."

"I didn't know that. I thought you were too busy doing rodeo to want to learn about running the ranch."

"I followed you everywhere. You brushed me off."

"I'm sorry, but you have to understand how much work is involved in running a place like this. And your mother? She worked her tail off to provide for you and your sister while you were growing up. We did go to your events while you were in high school. We went to every one. You didn't see us because we didn't think you wanted your friends to think you weren't cool. We saw you ride. We've even been to several of your bull riding events."

"You have?"

"Yes. We saw your ride in Oklahoma City."

Levi saw his mother standing in the doorway wringing her hands as tears rolled down her cheeks. "We love you, Curtis. You are our son. How could we not love you?"

"Why didn't you tell me you were there?"

"You were working. Bull riding is your job. You don't bother men while they're working."

Curt slowly sat back on the couch. "I feel like such an idiot. I've misjudged you both all these years thinking you didn't love me as much as Carolyn."

"Honey, we are so proud of you for being the man you are, you wouldn't understand. We are constantly telling folks about you, your life, and what you've accomplished," his mother said, putting her hands on his shoulders as she kissed the top of his head. "You are everything to us."

"Wow. I feel like shit. All these years I hated you for not being there for me, when you always were."

Levi saw Curt glance his direction and smile. The relationship between him and his parents had concluded in a happy ending. Now if they could get their happy ending, all would be perfect.

* * * *

Curt scooped up dinner with his spoon, letting the flavors explode on his tongue. He loved his mother's beef stew and rolls more than anything. "This is fantastic, Mom."

She smiled as she picked up his father's bowl to give him more of the delicious stew. "You are such a charmer, Curtis."

"So, Curtis, tell us about your relationship with Levi?"

Curt choked on his food. "What do you mean, Dad?"

"It's obvious there is something going on between you two, so spill it. We want the details."

After a few steadying breaths and a smile of encouragement from Levi, he said, "Levi and I are lovers. We've been together for several months now and we've fallen in love with each other. We are planning on making this a permanent relationship as soon as we can."

"You're getting married?"

The smile on his mother's face gave him the reassurance he needed to continue. "Yes." He turned to Levi. "At least I think that's where we are headed. We want to build a life together on Levi's ranch."

"How exciting!" His mother clapped her hands before coming around the table to hug both of them in turn.

"You're okay with me being gay?"

"You are who you are, Curtis. We don't pick your partner in life, you do. It's important for you to be happy. If Levi makes you happy, then so be it." His father clapped him on the shoulder. "We do want grandchildren someday from you, so you need to figure out how to make that happen, but you do what you need to for you."

"You have grandchildren from Carolyn."

"Yes, but she doesn't even know who the father of those kids are. We know how she's been milking you for money, and we want it to stop. She can learn to take care of herself from now on or get some money out of the men she's been shacking up with. Besides, you need to give me someone to leave this ranch to."

"The children we have may not be biologically mine though, if we adopt."

"They will be your children whether they have your genes or not. I don't care."

Curt shook his head and sighed as he reached over the table to grasp Levi's hand in his. "This has been such an eye opening day, I don't know how to absorb it all."

"I wish you could stay longer so we could get to know Levi more."

"We'll have to make an effort to come back to visit, that's all. We have a couple of months off from the circuit for now, so we'll make a trip out in a couple of weeks. It's only a half a day's drive," Levi answered, giving him no choice but to agree.

He didn't mind though. After today, he'd gladly visit his parents again. He had a lot of time to catch up on and he planned to spend every minute he could making up for it. "We need to get going,' Curt said, getting to his feet. "I don't want to get back home too late."

"Home." Levi smiled. "It has a nice ring to it."

"Our home."

He leaned in a kissed Levi on the mouth right there in front of his parents. When they separated, his mother was smiling so big, he thought her cheeks must hurt, and his father beamed as well.

"You two are too cute together. I'm so happy you found someone to love," his mother said as she hugged them both. "You two be careful driving home."

"Thanks, Mom. I love you."

"I love you too, Curtis. Call us when you get there."

"Sure."

He and Levi walked out to the truck and slid inside the cab. Levi slowly drove down the driveway, leaving his parent's home behind them.

"I can't believe how things went down. I feel like such an idiot."

"I'm glad it all got worked out."

"Yeah, me too, and to know they are supportive of us makes our relationship all the more sweet."

"Yes, it does."

"So when is the wedding?"

Epilogue

The day dawned bright and sunny for an October wedding.

Curt stood on one side of the row of chairs at the back, while Levi stood at the other side.

As the music started, they came together in the middle of the flower petal decorated walkway, and moved together toward the preacher standing before the archway at the end of the chairs.

Several hundred people had come to Levi's ranch to help them celebrate their union and their wedding in the eyes of God and the state of Oklahoma.

"Levi. Curt. Please join hands."

Levi took his hand as they stood side-by-side.

The preacher spoke of God, loving each other, and marriage as a sanctity of love, how they would grow old together, and how their union would be graced with the love of children—with a little help.

The crowd chuckled.

"I believe you two have written vows?"

"Yes," they said in unison as they turned to face each other.

"I'll go first," Curt said.

"You always were the more forceful one."

"You know it."

More laughter came from the crowd as they smiled at each other.

"Levi. Today I take you as my husband to love, honor, and cherish until death do us part. I will love you with my entire being forever. You are my soul, my life, and my life's partner. I know we will argue and I'll always win, but know that I love you no matter what." He slipped the wide gold band on Levi's left ring finger.

"Curtis. Today I take you as my husband to love, honor, and cherish until death do us part. Although we will argue, and no you won't win all the time, we will find love in our hearts for each other, any children we may be graced with, and our families. You are my life, my love, and my forever partner. I love you." Levi slipped a matching gold band on his left right finger.

They turned to face the preacher.

"By the power vested in me by the state of Oklahoma, I now pronounce you husband and husband. You may kiss your spouse."

He grabbed Levi by the lapels of his fancy tuxedo jacket, hauled him in close and smashed his mouth against Levi's lips. He'd been waiting for this day for months and now, Levi finally belonged to him in every sense of the word. They were forever bound in the eyes of God, the state of Oklahoma, but most importantly in each others' eyes.

When they finally separated, he whispered, "I love you."

Levi said, "I love you too."

"Ladies and gentlemen. I give you Mr. Levi Bond and his husband, Mr. Curtis Walsh."

The End

About the Author

Sandy Sullivan is a romance author, who, when not writing, spends her time with her husband Shaun on their farm in middle Tennessee. She loves to ride her horses, play with their dogs and relax on the porch, enjoying the rolling hills of her home south of Nashville. Country music is a passion of hers and she loves to listen to it while she writes.

She is an avid reader of romance novels and enjoys reading Nora Roberts, Jude Deveraux and Susan Wiggs. Finding new authors and delving into something different helps feed the need for literature. A registered nurse by education, she loves to help people and spread the enjoyment of romance to those around her with her novels. She loves cowboys so you'll find many of her novels have sexy men in tight jeans and cowboy boots.

Sandy's website
www.romancestorytime.com

Other books by Sandy

Love Me Once, Love Me Twice (Montana Cowboys 1)
Before the Night is Over (Montana Cowboys 2)
Two for the Price of One (Montana Cowboys 3)
Difficult Choices (Montana Cowboys 4)
Doctor Me Up (Montana Cowboys 5)
Stakin' His Claim
Country Minded Cougar
Meet Me in the Barn
Taming the Cougar
The Call of Duty Anthology
Five Hearts Anthology
Trouble With a Cowboy
Gotta Love a Cowboy
Make Mine a Cowboy (Cowboy Dreamin' 1)
Healing a Cowboy's Heart (Cowboy Dreamin' 2)
For the Love of a Cowboy (Cowboy Dreamin' 3)
Tempted by the Cowboy (Cowboy Dreamin' 4)
Forever Kind of Cowboy (Cowboy Dreamin' 5)
Kiss Me, Cowboy (Cowboy Dreamin' 6)
A Cowboy and a Country Song (Cowboy Dreamin' 7)

Secret Cravings Publishing
www.secretcravingspublishing.com

www.ingramcontent.com/pod-product-compliance
Lightning Source LLC
Chambersburg PA
CBHW060144130626
46556CB00006B/2485